To Jes
'Always on

ELVIS THE ASTRONAUT

BY

ROBERT WELLS

Elvisly Yours
Robert

Published by New Generation Publishing in 2024

Copyright © Robert Wells 2024

First Edition

The author asserts the moral right under the Copyright, Designs and Patents Act 1988 to be identified as the author of this work.

All Rights reserved. No part of this publication may be reproduced, stored in a retrieval system or transmitted, in any form or by any means without the prior consent of the author, nor be otherwise circulated in any form of binding or cover other than that which it is published and without a similar condition being imposed on the subsequent purchaser.

ISBN: 9781835633878

New Generation Publishing
www.newgeneration-publishing.com

CONTENTS

Elvis the Astronaut	5
Springsteen's Song for Elvis	19
The Elusive Hawaiian-shirted Pimpernel	29
The Return of Mae West	42
The Chicken Liberation Army	58
The World's Rarest Animal	71
The Presley Turnip Patch	80
The Tupelo Thunderbolt	88
A Tsunami of Elvises	100
The Retirement Home for Elvis Tribute Artists	111
Too Much Monkey Business	122
That's All Right	136

ELVIS THE ASTRONAUT

Ostensibly, Colonel Parker should be busy going through the pile of letters on his desk which have been sent by charities and other worthy causes seeking help from Elvis. Dozens are delivered every day to Graceland; however, the Colonel deems them to be of low priority, on a par with suppliers' invoices, in how he manages the affairs of Elvis and EPCP Enterprises.

When no more letters can be crammed into the cupboard where they're kept, such as on this occasion, he knows he must go through them. It's a noisy routine, usually accompanied by the gnashing of teeth, mutterings, and outbursts of mocking laughter. Almost all the correspondence ends up in the 'out sack' which is positioned next to his desk.

Occasionally he'll read out a particularly choice item to Bubba, his assistant, such as a request for any clothes that can be sent to a rummage sale.

"They probably want me to send them his ten-thousand-dollar gold lame suit because he hasn't worn it for ten years," he roars, his face bright red with indignation.

But this time things are different. Bubba is intrigued, because he seems to be using the letters to make paper aeroplanes, although he has yet to launch one across the office. When he cannot contain his curiosity any longer, he asks what he's doing. He's shocked by the answer.

"I'm trying my hand at origami," he replies. "Do you know that the top executives of very large Japanese corporations spend a lot of time doing origami as a way of relieving stress and helping them become better businessmen? I thought it might help me run the affairs of the world's greatest entertainer. I took it up after I got book on origami as a free gift with my last order of cigars from Walmart. You should see the pictures of some of the things they've made from a single piece of paper, like a charging elephant or the Empire State Building."

He holds up a shape he has been working on for the last few minutes. "What do you think it is, Bubba?"

He hasn't a clue; it looks a bit of a mess, but since origami is a Japanese art, he takes a guess and suggests it's Godzilla.

His boss sighs deeply and shakes his head. "For goodness' sake," he snaps. "Can't you tell it's a rabbit!"

His young assistant realises he's dropped a clanger. "Sorry, sir. Now that the cigar smoke has started to clear, I can tell that it's a rabbit. Silly me! From this distance, and through the smoke, it looked at first as if it had only one ear and a long tail."

At that moment the phone rings and the Colonel, already busy folding another charity letter, signals to his assistant that he should deal with the call.

"No, I'm sorry but Colonel Parker is not available. He's taking part in a Japanese management training programme for the senior executives of very large corporations. Is there a message I can give him?

"Excuse me, but did you say Nassau? I'm Colonel Parker's assistant and I can assure you that he doesn't have any offshore accounts in the Bahamas or anywhere else. All our banking arrangements are handled by the Bank of Jefferson Davis in Richmond.

"I'm sorry but will you repeat that. You're from NASA, as in the National Aeronautics and Space Administration. Right, I understand, and you'd like to speak to Colonel Parker about his idea of sending Elvis into space.

"You want me to tell him you're very interested, and he should call you as soon as possible to arrange a meeting. Who should he ask for? You, and you're the Administrator and you're in charge of NASA. Got it. I'm sure he'll be in touch as soon as possible."

He tries to stay calm as he replaces the receiver. In the years he's worked for the Colonel, Bubba reckons he's become shockproof to some of the schemes he's dreamed up to promote Elvis's career, while at the same time making more and more money for himself as well as his client. But Elvis the astronaut – this is off the scale.

He mentions that the call was from NASA, and they'd like to meet him to discuss his plan to put Elvis in a rocket and blast him off into space. "Pardon me for asking, sir, but does Elvis know about this?"

"No, not yet. But he'll love it because he's a great patriot and he'll be doing it for his country."

"But isn't it highly dangerous?"

"It's a lot safer than driving down Union Avenue on a Saturday night," he comments. "Let's go and see Elvis and give him the good news."

They find him sitting on an exercise bike that has been set up in a corner of the Jungle Room; however, he is resting rather than pedalling, and gazing wistfully out of the window. Picked out in blue crystals on the front of his tracksuit top is the slogan 'Pain is Gain'. A bucket of popcorn dangles from the handlebars. His relaxed demeanour and the absence of any signs of physical exertion makes the Colonel wonder when, or if, he's going to start. Elvis's old friend and gofer-in-chief Charlie Hodge is sitting down, holding a clipboard on which nothing has been written apart from the date.

"I see you're getting in shape for your next season at the International," notes the Colonel. "Excellent! And how are his scores coming along, Charlie? Getting better day by day, are they?"

Charlie hurriedly drops the clipboard into the front pocket of his pinafore where it cannot be seen before answering that Elvis will soon resemble a top athlete ready to compete in the next Olympic Games.

"Which event will that be?" he inquires.

Charlie frowns, not knowing how to reply, and inwardly wishing he'd never opened his mouth.

Once they have moved to sit in the armchairs in another part of the Jungle Room, Colonel Parker apologises to Elvis for interrupting his workout, saying something has come up which means he may well have to postpone his upcoming season in Las Vegas.

Elvis suppresses a smile. "Tut tut. Just when I was doing so well with my new fitness regime," he sighs regretfully.

"He's in great shape," adds Charlie loyally. "He reminds me of that guy Charles Atlas who used to kick sand in the faces of the kids on the beach."

"There's no need to be disappointed, son," Colonel Parker tells him. "Please carry on with the workouts. They're going to be very useful for what we've got planned. I've postponed your new season of shows because something of international importance has come up, and I know you're going to be very excited."

Elvis is more nervous than excited, not knowing what his manager is going to pull out of his hat.

Colonel Parker executes a twirl with his cigar, as if he were a majorette, before announcing in his best carnival barker style: "You're going to be the Rocket Man. Yes, Elvis, we're sending you into outer space."

Elvis has turned to stone. He sits in his chair, eyes and mouth wide open, as rigid and mute as a statue.

He continues: "You're going to be the first entertainer in space, a star among the stars, the first to perform a show while circling the world, watched by billions of your fans!"

Elvis emerges from his state of shock to ask why.

"Because, son, it's never been done before and you're always the Number One. And because it will save NASA's space programme. And because, I must admit, it will make us a lot of money."

"But Colonel, sir, I'm not qualified to fly one of those rockets!" he protests.

"You can do it, King," interjects Charlie. "And I'll be up there with you, just like when we're on stage together."

Colonel Parker concludes the meeting by saying, "I promise you won't have to do anything but sing. We're due in D.C. in a couple of days' time for a meeting with NASA to finalise the details."

On arrival at the headquarters of NASA in Washington D.C. security checks are waived aside for Elvis and Colonel Parker. It's the King, the most famous man in the world: Why would they need to vet him? They're applauded through the lobby to the lifts, while the PA system thoughtfully plays the theme of *2001: A Space Odyssey* which heralds every stage appearance of Elvis.

For the occasion he's wearing a metallic silver jumpsuit designed by Bernard Lansky, with an image of the cartoon character Flash Gordon on the chest, a rocket blasting off to the stars on the cape, and a large belt buckle that looks like a space buggy.

Elvis pauses by the lifts, as if he's just remembered something; he removes a ring, walks back across the lobby, and presents it to the receptionist, who squeals with delight, and then faints. By now more people have joined the crowd who have gathered to see him and the din from the hooting and hollering is deafening. It's all so unlike the usual laboratory-like atmosphere of the building.

In the meeting room, sitting opposite Elvis and the Colonel, along the length of the table must be 20 people, most of them in suits, and some in white lab coats; among them are top brass from the Army and Air Force, with enough gold braid on their uniforms to be of interest to Fort Knox.

The Administrator, who is sitting in the centre of this line-up, goes through the preliminaries of welcoming them and says they'd like to hear more about why NASA should launch Elvis into space.

He continues: "We're privileged that the world's greatest entertainer has joined us today for this meeting and to volunteer his services for this historic enterprise. America is proud of you, Elvis." He coughs, and looks a little embarrassed, before adding that they'd all like to get his autograph after the meeting.

The Colonel pats his briefcase and tells them: "It just so happens that I've brought some photos which Elvis will gladly sign for you."

He explains that since man landed on the moon in 1969, interest in the space programme has waned with the public. That feat, wonderful though it was, is now viewed as the pinnacle, and having been achieved, what more is there to do? Mr and Mrs America have switched off. Consequently, a lack of interest among the voters has resulted in a lack of dollars being committed by the government to the space programme.

As evidence of this decline, he points out that more than twice as many people watched *Elvis: Aloha from Hawaii* than saw Neil Armstrong land on the moon.

"That says it all," he adds. "We need to find a way of putting the space programme back in the forefront of the minds of Americans."

There is a chorus of murmuring accompanied by the shaking of heads of the boffins and the military top brass.

"The exploration of space is a race that America must win," declares the Administrator. "For our nation's future security as well as the advancement of human knowledge about the universe. So please tell us, Colonel Parker, and Elvis, what are your ideas to turn the tide?"

"Your answer is sitting right here," he declares, placing a fatherly hand on Elvis's shoulder. "You need to combine the two: Space travel and Elvis. Trust me: it's a guaranteed, twenty-four carat success."

The Administrator looks puzzled and says he's not sure what the Colonel means. "Elvis is the King of Rock and Roll and a movie star. But he's not an astronaut."

"He doesn't need to be," declares the Colonel. "That's right, isn't it, Elvis?"

"Huh huh."

"Here's how it will work. Everybody can relate to Elvis, the embodiment of the American Dream. You send him up in a rocket, and everybody will switch on their TVs. While it circles the earth, the world's greatest entertainer will perform a special, one-man show that'll be watched by billions of people. And that's mission accomplished.

"In one go you'll reconnect with ordinary people who'll be reminded that space travel is not remote and inaccessible. It's relevant, and because it can beam Elvis into almost every home on the planet, it is something that touches the lives of everybody."

"Aren't we in danger of turning NASA into a sort of Ed Sullivan Show," sneers a five-star general.

Elvis interjects: "Excuse me, sir, but that show did my career a whole lotta good!"

The general blushes at his faux pas and remains silent for the rest of the meeting.

Colonel Parker says that he'd like to discuss his marketing ideas to maximise coverage of Elvis's launch into space. While he unwraps one of his Walmart cigars, a four-star general uses his baton to push a NASA ashtray towards him. From its weight he can tell it's made of lead crystal, and it would add class to the home he shares with Mrs Parker. He makes a mental note to slide it into his briefcase, perhaps at the end of the meeting, when everybody is leaving, and nobody is looking.

He runs through the initial media blitz, to be followed by the sale of merchandising. He comments that he's already been in touch with his international partners (he means the sweat shops he uses in Soweto and Bangladesh). Phase Three will be the launch party at Cape Canaveral.

The NASA representatives look at each other, grim-faced. But they know they've decided to ride the tiger and now there is no getting off. As they get to their feet to leave the meeting, the Colonel shouts "Whoa!" and asks them to resume their seats.

"It's funny, isn't it, just when you think you've finished, how easy it is to overlook something really important." He looks along the line of the blank faces sitting opposite him and tells them: "We forgotten to talk about the fees! Can you believe it!"

"What fees?" demands the Administrator.

"The fees for Elvis and me."

"But as I understood it, you volunteered to do this so that, in your own words, you could save the space programme."

"Elvis has had to sacrifice so much," he declares. He has learned his lines well and proceeds to list them on the podgy fingers of his hands: A record-breaking season at The International Hotel; a new movie with top Hollywood producer Hal Wallis; a new album of self-penned songs... Eventually he runs out of fingers and thumbs. Apart from the season at the International, Elvis has never heard of any of the others.

"What sort of figures are you talking about?" ask the Administrator.

The Colonel thinks of a number and adds a nought at the end for luck.

When they hear it, several people at the table nearly fall off their chairs, including Elvis.

When the negotiations are completed, his manager asks one of the boffins if he can borrow his white lab coat. It is a stunt he's pulled before, usually at the conclusion of a particularly good deal. On other occasions he's used a tablecloth and a napkin. Elvis groans at the pantomime that is about to take place.

Colonel Parker writes down the key points of the contract that has just been agreed on the back of the lab coat, which he folds up and pops into his briefcase, while everyone else in the room watches in disbelief.

He removes a sheath of photographs. "Anyone like an autograph?" he says brightly.

"No charge," adds Elvis.

Priscilla calls a family meeting at a time when Colonel Parker is away from Graceland to discuss Elvis's plan to climb into a rocket and perform a concert in outer space.

"Honestly, I've never heard of anything so ridiculous in my whole life! You're the King of Rock and Roll, you're a movie star, but you're not an astronaut. So please tell us why you want to do it."

"Well, honey, it's never been done before," he replies. "Basically, it's an extension of *Aloha from Hawaii*, which was broadcast via satellite to some parts of the world. This time, I'll be performing to all my fans as I circle the earth in a rocket."

"But it's so dangerous," she protests. "You're risking your life. Think of your family first."

"Colonel Parker says it's safer than driving down Union Avenue on a Saturday night," Elvis replies.

Vernon, who has always been his manager's biggest supporter in the family, comments: "You can count on the Colonel; he'll have looked into this very carefully and got a watertight contract that makes sure Elvis is safe."

Priscilla hits back: "How much danger will that fat felon be in! He'll have a contract that gives him half of all the revenues without having to get up from behind his desk."

Charlie Hodge, Elvis's old friend and gofer-in-chief, tells of his distress that for the first time Elvis will be performing without him by his side. "I'm heartbroken," he says, dabbing his eyes and blowing his nose on a yellow duster he keeps in his pinafore pocket. "They say it's a one-man capsule, but I'm not very big and I bet they could squeeze me in if they really tried."

The meeting ends with Minnie Mae, Elvis's grandmother, telling them, "Ah'm a-sayin' this: if'n the boy don't come back ter earth, then me an' Grandpappy Hood's ole buffalo gun will be a-waitin' fer the Colonel."

The first teaser ads appear on billboards and in newspapers, magazines and on TV screens. Against a background of a night sky and hundreds of twinkling stars, the headline asks: 'Who's the brightest star'? At the bottom is a strapline that declares: 'Watch this space'. The play of words on 'space', dreamt up by Bubba, his young assistant, particularly appeals to the Colonel who, of course, claims the credit.

The media blitz continues a week later with the announcement that Elvis will be launched in a NASA rocket for the first concert to be performed from outer space. It adds, although this is news to Elvis, that he will also be carrying out important research work.

"What am I supposed to do?" he asks his manager. "I've not been given any training."

"Nothing," he tells him. "It's just PR."

"But what if anybody asks me?"

"Tell them it's highly sensitive and very confidential. You've seen the file and it's stamped 'Top Secret' in red capital letters. Your lips are sealed."

"Right."

The climax of the Colonel's marketing programme is the launch party at Cape Canaveral, which he'd hoped to turn into a replica of Coney Island, with the help of some of his old carny friends. To his fury, NASA won't countenance the idea, feeling it will cheapen the proceedings. "Cheap!" he explodes at the indignity of such a word being used. However, they agree to a few stalls selling his specially produced merchandise of sweaters, T-shirts, socks, Elvis bobbleheads in a space suit and Elvis dolls, also in a space suit.

Space junk is how it is all described by NASA's own marketing team.

Disappointingly, the origami paper figures of Elvis do not sell well.

"Perhaps it's an art form that's not yet fully appreciated," says his assistant, Bubba, trying to console him. But he dares not ask who made them in case it's the Colonel himself.

President Nixon, gauging that his popularity with voters will be considerably boosted by attending the launch and being photographed with Elvis, decides to go, together with his wife, Pat, and their two daughters. Government business virtually ceases since so many senators, congressmen and congresswomen think the same and want to be there, too.

Among the Hollywood and showbiz royalty who attend are Liberace and Mae West, each vying in their different ways, to attract the attention of the NASA Administrator to secure their spot as the next entertainer in space.

Elvis, dressed in his space suit and with his helmet tucked under his arm, joins President Nixon on the rostrum that's draped in the American flag, for the official farewell ceremony. The President speaks of the unique fusion of important scientific research and entertainment that Elvis will perform on his historic mission into space.

"Both tasks will be of great benefit to mankind," he declares. "America, and the rest of the world, salute you, Elvis."

Elvis says he is honoured to serve his country in any way he can before getting into the elevator that takes him into the rocket.

The technicians strap him into his chair and remind him that he'll be told when it is safe to release himself and move around. They point out the machine that will play the backing tracks he's requested for his performance and run through again how to operate it.

Finally, they show him a big red button which he should not touch under any circumstances unless there's an emergency because it will immediately release the capsule from the rocket.

"That means it could land anywhere, instead of where it's scheduled, which is in the sea off Cape Canaveral," they tell him. "And we don't want that to happen, do we, and disappoint everybody who'll be there to welcome you back!"

"You mean this button," says Elvis, pretending to push it.

"That's the one!" and they all laugh.

Weightlessness is a strange, wonderful, euphoric feeling for Elvis, as he hovers like a bird, exploring the inside of the capsule. Having been told he can now leave his chair, the team at Mission Control advise him to get used to the sensation before going live and starting one of his concert performances.

Elvis wants to take a little more time enjoying the sensation of flight and learning how to gain more control over his movements. Using his legs like pistons he propels himself from one side of the capsule to the other. He pretends he's been transformed into his favourite childhood comic book superhero, Captain Marvel Jnr. Such exhilaration! Such fun!

"Sorry to interrupt, but it's time to start your concert," Cape Canaveral tells him.

"Okay."

He glides across to switch on the machine with his backing music and begins the show in the traditional way that won't disappoint all the fans who are watching him: *C C Rider* is followed by a medley of *Mystery Train* and *Tiger Man*.

"My next song is one I've never performed before, but it seems kind of appropriate because of the way I'm floating around here in my capsule. It's called *Rubber Ball*."

As he sings, he propels himself back and forth across the interior of the capsule, gaining momentum each time, in keeping with the lyrics with lines such as '*Rubber ball, I come bouncin' back to you'*. Then comes disaster. It must have been the high from the adrenalin rush of his performance that causes him not to notice the emergency red button. Or maybe he'd just forgotten about it. But as he is about to push off back across the capsule, he accidentally treads on it. There is a huge explosion, a blinding flash of light, and then blackness as the capsule is catapulted from the rocket into outer space to begin its downward trajectory towards earth.

Elvis straps himself tightly into his chair, cursing himself for his carelessness, and wondering where in the world he'll land. He guesses it won't be Cape Canaveral, but somewhere warm would be nice.

Back on earth there is pandemonium. The team at Mission Control hope they know what happened – that an emergency or a systems failure somehow caused the capsule to be ejected from the rocket and they need to work frantically to plot where it might come down. That there could be a more disastrous reason is too terrible to contemplate.

Elvis's fans stunned that the King has suddenly disappeared from their screens, literally with a bang, and not knowing what has happened, but fearing the worst, pour on to the streets like rivers that have burst their banks; many of them bring their most precious Elvis artefacts – an album, a teddy bear, or a heart-shaped red satin cushion. Already there is talk amongst them of organising a march on Washington D.C. to demand a public inquiry to find out who is to blame – the President, the Government, NASA, his record label RCA, Colonel Parker…

In their despair, they need the solace of a victim.

Priscilla has locked herself in her room with their daughter, Lisa Marie, desperate to keep her from watching the news unfold on TV.

President Nixon wants to make a broadcast to announce that he is taking personal control of the search for Elvis. His aides warn him that it is a high-risk strategy. If they find Elvis alive and well, then he'll be a hero; if not, and he was the person who was seen waving him off into space, then he will become the most reviled American since Benedict Arnold. Boom or bust? What to do?

"Somehow we've managed to lose the most famous man in the world, on my watch," he groans, wiping away the perspiration erupting on to his brow, like a spa.

He knows he must do it and tells TV viewers: "Wherever the capsule lands, and I do mean anywhere on this earth, we will go there and bring Elvis home. Of course, we pray that he is safe. Once that is done, I'll report back to the American people and his fans around the world on what happened."

Nixon has already received a call from HM The Queen's private secretary, who tells him: "Her Majesty is most anxious about Elvis and asks to be kept fully informed of all developments." He adds that she is sending a personal message to his family.

Colonel Parker rings Bubba at Graceland, saying he is with RCA in Nashville, trying to organise the possible release of a memorial album.

His assistant is shocked. "How can you, sir! That's so callous! We don't even know yet what has happened to Elvis."

"It's business," he replies. "I need to be ready for any eventuality. It's what he would have wanted."

"I'm sure that what Elvis wanted is to be back home," retorts Bubba.

"It's what we all hope for," responds the Colonel. "We're also working on a compilation album to celebrate if it's good news. It'll be called 'The King is Back'."

Bubba advises him that it would be wise for him to stay away from Graceland for the time being. Minnie Mae is sitting in a rocking chair on the portico with a big shotgun across her lap, saying she is waiting for the Colonel to show up.

"Me?"

"Yes, sir. Apparently, she blames you for what's happened to Elvis."

"Why me? I'll come and have a chat with her and explain things."

"I really wouldn't. She looks mean; she tells me she's done with talking and her trigger finger is itching."

Elvis is in luck and gets his wish for the space capsule to land somewhere warm; it splashes down in the southern Pacific Ocean near a remote island which is part of the Kingdom of Tonga. The sky and the sea are a flawless blue colour, and he is dazzled by the reflection of the sun on the silver sands of the beach, fringed by tall palm trees. Having earlier taken off his space suit, he wades ashore in white cotton overalls, feeling like Robinson Crusoe after he was shipwrecked.

He stands there, hands on hips, with the surf lapping around his feet, admiring the view, and oh so glad to be alive. He'd feared the worst as the space capsule plunged towards earth; he was helpless, because there was nothing that he could do to change the outcome; he had to wait and accept his fate. Now it looks as if he's found paradise.

Wouldn't it be great, he thinks to himself, if he had somehow landed in Hawaii. It causes him to start softly singing *Can't Help Falling in Love*.

Suddenly a group of 20 natives burst out of the trees and race down the beach towards him, yelling and waving clubs and spears above their heads. Elvis shouts his battle cry of 'Kiai' and goes into his karate kill stance, his hands poised like axes, ready to strike.

When they are about 10 yards away the natives stop and peer at him, before going into a huddle. He can't make any sense of what they're saying, but some of them point at him, and a couple of times he thinks he hears his name being mentioned.

One man, presumably their leader, leaves the group and walks cautiously towards him; he points his finger at him, and says, "Elvis?"

He jabs his finger in his chest, nods his head, and replies, "Yes, I'm Elvis!"

The leader falls to his knees, followed by the rest of the group, and together they bow their heads towards the sand, before standing up and lifting their arms to the sky and shouting "Elvis!"

Moments ago, he feared they were going to kill him; now they are escorting him away from the beach as if he were royalty.

He remembers something that Colonel Parker once said about fame: Elvis is the only man who can walk down any street anywhere in the world and be recognised. Not the President, not the Pope, not the Queen. Only Elvis. You can add to that a remote island somewhere in the middle of an ocean.

They take him to a collection of huts in a clearing in the trees; in the centre is a conical-shaped hut that is much bigger than the others. The only illumination is provided by a hole in the roof through which the smoke from the fire escapes, and the flap of the door being left open. In the murk he can make out some 20 men, women and children squatting on the floor of the hut who bow towards him and murmur "Elvis". As a 'jungle room', with its mud floor and bare walls, it compares very poorly with the one back home in Graceland in terms of comfort.

An old man sitting in a chair near the fire stands up and motions for him to take his place.

One of the other men goes to a box in the corner and takes out two copies of the Hollywood Reporter, wrapped in palm leaves, which he shows to Elvis. They date from 1956 and there are stories and pictures of him on the front and inside pages; although a little frayed and faded, they're in surprisingly good condition.

From this man, who speaks a few words of English, but mainly through mime, he learns that many years ago a boat came to the island and a sailor told them of a man called Elvis who was the King, the greatest singer in the world; he hoped that one day they would see him, too, and know why he was the King. He'd left behind the newspapers so that they would recognise him. Since then, they've been treated as precious relics of the King who might one day visit their island. Today a miracle has happened – he's arrived in his strange-looking boat and waded ashore.

The islanders, all of whom are now squeezed inside the hut, want him to sing. For them it will be proof of his royalty. He promises that once it gets dark, and the stars are in the sky, that is the time when he will entertain them. They grin, clap their hands and chatter excitedly among themselves, impatient for him to begin.

For his concert, he'll include a couple of songs from *Blue Hawaii*, since they have a South Seas feel; but he wants the islanders to experience the excitement of his live shows, even though he'll be performing without his band and backing singers. He decides to start with his usual opening number, *C C Rider* and include *Burning Love* and *Suspicious Minds*.

Meanwhile, back at Mission Control, they have determined that the space capsule splashed down somewhere near the island of Tonga and President Nixon, as Commander-in-Chief, orders an aircraft carrier of the Pacific Fleet, with its complement of jets and helicopters, to head there at full speed to search for Elvis.

Too soon, Elvis realises his brief time in paradise is at an end. A US Navy helicopter is circling overhead, having identified the space capsule moored on the beach. He emerges from the trees, surrounded by the islanders, to wave to the helicopter. The crew immediately radio back to the aircraft carrier from where a message that Elvis has been found is relayed to the White House and NASA.

President Nixon, having spoken first to Priscilla at Graceland and then Buckingham Palace, calls a press conference in the Oval Office to announce that Elvis has been found alive and well on a remote Pacific Island.

Normally a perpetual worrier, for once the President is a happy man. Having led the search for Elvis, and then being the one to announce that Elvis was on his way back home, should be enough to guarantee his place in the hearts of the American people and victory for the Republican party in the 1976 presidential election. Maybe, they'll be so grateful they'll make him Emeritus President for life.

As Elvis walks towards the helicopter, the islanders wail and pull at his arms to try to drag him back towards the village. He struggles free, points at the helicopter, and flaps his arms to show them he must fly away. Saddened by their distress, he tells them through his interpreter he will return and next time he'll bring his queen.

Once they understand this, the mood changes, and a buzz of excitement runs through all 50 islanders on the beach. They smile and hug each other. At a signal, every man, woman, and child gets down on one knee and starts to whirl their right arms round and round like windmills, just like they've seen their king do.

Then they stand up and chant, "Hunka, hunka; Hunka, hunka; Hunka, hunka," as they walk with Elvis to the helicopter.

SPRINGSTEEN'S SONG FOR ELVIS

Colonel Parker is in a bad mood. He's had his right arm put in a sling by Dr Nick, Elvis's personal physician, to ease the Repetitive Strain Injury caused by, he's been told, spending too much time pulling on the levers of gaming machines. Knowing what's likely to happen, Dr Nick has warned him that unless he stops playing, the same thing will affect his left arm.

But the Colonel is addicted to one-arm bandits; they are one of the principal staples of his life, along with food, drink, cigars, and making deals. He keeps one next to his desk in his office at Graceland and he thinks he has come up with a solution to the problem of how to play; while still sitting in his chair, he attempts to depress the handle of the gaming machine with the hook of a walking stick which he holds in his left hand.

It is proving to be a very awkward manoeuvre, and it keeps sliding off the handle; as his level of irritation increases, so does the number and volume of the curses that he utters.

"Sorry to interrupt, sir, but I wonder if I might mention this letter to you," says Bubba, his assistant, who decides against asking if he has won anything yet. From his mood, he guesses not.

"Dammit!" roars a frustrated Colonel Parker, furiously flinging the walking stick across the office in the general direction of the coat stand. "Can't you see how busy I am! This had better be important!"

"It's from Bruce Springsteen and he says he's written a song for Elvis."

"Who's he?" He looks bewildered.

"I'm surprised you've not heard of him, sir. He's very popular and great things are predicted of him. They say he's the future of rock and roll."

"Ridiculous!" he sneers. "How can that be? Elvis is the King – the past, the present and the future of rock and roll. What's this song called?"

"He doesn't say, sir, and he hasn't enclosed a tape of it. According to his letter, he wants to go through it personally with Elvis."

Colonel Parker affects to roar with laughter, as if he's just been told the funniest joke in the world. "Priceless! He should take up being a comedian. Doesn't he know that Hill & Range, the music publishers, supply songs to Elvis. That's the deal, that's how the system works, and everybody benefits."

Apart from Elvis, thinks Bubba, since most of the songs sent to him by the music publishers are pretty dreadful.

"File the letter in the 'Thanks But No Thanks' Songs file, along with the others that have been sent in by people hoping Elvis will make them rich and famous by singing one of them."

"If you don't mind my saying, sir, Springsteen's songs are very good, like *Born to Run*, for example, and we have nothing to lose. Remember, Elvis is looking for material for his next album and RCA insist it must feature new songs. It mustn't be another compilation, like the previous three."

His boss struggles to unwrap the cellophane from a Walmart cigar with his left hand, and only succeeds in snapping it in half; undeterred, he lights one of the stubs. He should acknowledge there is justice in the remarks of his assistant, but he tries to uphold his position by saying that he should have sent a tape.

Bubba tells him: "Springsteen says in his letter that this is the second song he's written for Elvis. He sent a tape with the first one, but he waited and waited, and when he heard nothing, he gave the song to the Pointer Sisters."

"Who are they?"

"They're also very popular, sir, and the song went to Number Two in the Hot 100."

The Colonel gazes at the nicotine-stained ceiling of his office for a while, as if deep in thought, and Bubba begins to wonder if what he has said has caused him to change his mind about the song. It doesn't look like it, because he tells Bubba that he's giving up using the walking stick to operate his gaming machine. He has a new idea. He instructs him to go to the stables and get a piece of rope; one end will be tied to the lever and the other to his foot, allowing him to operate it while leaving his good hand free. "Genius," he adds.

Later that day, on returning to the office, Bubba finds that the gaming machine has toppled over, and Colonel Parker is lying in a heap on the floor by his desk. Since he's one of the fattest men in America, getting him up and back into his chair will need a team of people, maybe even a block and tackle, so he heads for the Jungle Room to enlist the help of Elvis, Red and Sonny West, and Charlie Hodge, who are there watching TV and drinking beer.

Having told them what has happened, and that it was probably caused by the Colonel yanking too hard with his foot, he waits until they have all finished laughing.

"Picking him up will be one helluva job," grins Elvis. "Can we phone Clark Kent?"

"Are we covered by medical insurance?" asks Charlie, his oldest friend and chief gofer. "We could do some serious damage to ourselves."

Bubba suggests that Dr Nick, Elvis's personal physician, should accompany them in case the Colonel is injured.

It's like trying to move a beached walrus as the guys, shouting "to me, to you," struggle to lift him, while the Colonel grimaces and cries "Ow!" and "You're hurting me!"

Once they have got him into a sitting position on the floor, Elvis calls for a rest. They send for reinforcements and with the extra help of Elvis's hair stylist Larry Geller and Lamar Fike, they're finally able to hoist him into his chair.

Dr Nick examines him and make some notes on his clipboard. In his white suit, shiny black shirt with basset hound ears collar, and a gold medallion around his neck, he looks as if he is on his way to a disco afterwards.

"It's bad news, I'm afraid," he announces to the room, with a sad shake of his head. "His left wrist is badly sprained, probably caused by him trying to break his fall, and it needs to be put in a sling. And after the shock and all the effort expended in getting up again, he probably should have a period of complete rest."

"No, I can't do that! I must take care of business, but how am I to work with no hands?" complains Colonel Parker, although he's relieved that the doctor's favourite treatment – enemas – has not been mentioned.

"EPCP Enterprises needs me at the helm," he continues, "ever ready to steer the ship away from troubled waters. The business cannot afford for me to take any time off."

Elvis points out that he can talk, and he has an assistant to help him.

"You'll still be on the bridge," says Bubba, seeking to reassure him, "and I'm sure it'll only be for a short time. I mean, what can go wrong?"

Elvis is sitting in the Jungle Room, plunking in a desultory way on his Fender bass, musing on what songs to include on his new album. To make life as easy as possible for him, RCA have set up a state-of-the-art recording studio in the Jungle Room. That was a week ago and so far, he's recorded a couple of songs, *Hurt*, and an old country standard, *Blue Eyes Crying in the Rain*.

"They're good songs, but the bottom line is that I'm recycling the hits of other artists," he grumbles. "I hate what Hill & Range is sending me, and what the Colonel wants me to do. I need brand new material."

The session musicians turn up each day, but Elvis shrugs his shoulders to indicate nothing doing, and tells them to come back tomorrow. They do, but more dispirited with each passing day. Meanwhile, some of the guys are moaning – not within Elvis's hearing, of course – that they resent the intrusion of the recording studio. They like the Jungle Room as it was, somewhere they could watch TV, drink beer, read the funny papers, and fall asleep.

"Bubba tells me that Bruce Springsteen has written a new song for me but guess what, the Colonel turned it down flat," he tells Charlie.

"He's on tour and he's doing a show in Memphis tonight," remarks his old friend.

"Great, because I'm going to go, take in the show, see what he's like, and find out about this song he's written."

Charlie looks aghast. "No, King, you can't! It's too big a risk! Think of the security!"

"I'll be fine, I'll go in disguise."

"What if you're recognised, even if you wear your airline pilot sunglasses and yachting cap! The fans will become so excited, wanting to greet you, that it'll turn into a riot. And what about poor old Bruce Springsteen? What will he think, standing up there on stage, and seeing all the fans ignoring the show because you're there?"

"But, Charlie, what about the song? I need it. It could be a game-changer for me."

His old friend takes off his floral pinafore that he wears when he does the housework at Graceland, folds it up, and pops it into a drawer. "Here's what we'll do, King. I'll go instead. I probably won't be recognised, so there won't be a fuss, and I'll have a quiet word with him and sort everything out."

Meanwhile, Bubba walks into Colonel Parker's office and immediately turns round and walks out again, so that he can cram a handkerchief into his mouth to stop himself laughing out loud at what he's just seen.

Sitting at his desk, his boss looks like the Big Bird character from the children's TV programme *Sesame Street*. He's the same big, bulbous shape, he's wearing a bright yellow Hawaiian shirt and his arms, tucked into slings, resemble tiny wings. To complete the picture, he's smoking a cigar that's been fitted into a stand, made from two metal coat hangers.

"Did you get that from Schwab's, sir?" Bubba asks innocently, indicating the contraption on the desk.

"No, Vernon made it for me. The only snag is how to light my cigar. But I've come up with the answer. I've asked Schwab's to put a Bunsen burner on my desk and fit it to a gas cylinder."

Bubba is horrified. "But, sir, that sounds very dangerous. If anything goes wrong, you'll be sitting next to a bomb, one that could demolish Graceland and kill us all. And just because you want to light a cigar!"

"Well, what do you suggest?"

"We can put a bell on the floor by your desk and you can step on it to summon someone to come. Or we can hire somebody as your cigar lighter assistant. But please let me call Schwab's and cancel the order. I'm sure we'll all sleep a lot easier knowing that Graceland won't be blown up."

Colonel Parker looks disappointed and says he'll consider it. "Anything else?" he adds.

"I was wondering, sir, if I might have this evening off."

"Will that be in addition to the Sunday afternoons that you always have off?"

"Well, er, yes."

He flaps his two arms in slings at him, like a seal in a circus asking for a fish. "Oh dear, given my current predicament, you can see your request could not have come at a worst time. I'm not an unreasonable man, and I'll allow it, but I hope you don't think I'm being unfair if I take it out of your salary."

Bubba reminds him that under the terms of his apprenticeship, he receives free board and lodging at Graceland and out-of-pocket expenses – but no salary.

"No harm done, then," he acknowledges. "What will you be doing? Taking some extra classes in business administration?"

"No, sir, I thought I'd go to the Bruce Springsteen concert in Memphis."
"Why?"
"I want to go and see for myself what he's like on stage."

The first hour and a half of Springsteen's show in Memphis is very rock and roll, raucous and frenetic, but he's done a couple of slower, acoustic numbers, things have quietened down, and Charlie thinks now might be a good time to speak to him.

He reckons he won't be able to get to see him in his dressing room after the show; either security will bar the way or, like Elvis, he'll leave the building as soon as he's finished. His best chance is the direct approach – to climb on to the stage during his act and have a quick word with him on Elvis's behalf. At least, that's how Charlie sees it.

Dressed in the white jumpsuit that he usually wears when he performs with Elvis, he sets off down the aisle; nobody notices him until he walks up the steps at the side of the stage.

He approaches Springsteen who doesn't seem in anyway disconcerted; this sort of thing happens a lot at his shows, and he carries on singing. Two large security men, in bulging suits and shaven heads, run on stage and lift Charlie off his feet. As they carry him away horizontally, like a roll of carpet, between them, Charlie calls out: "I only wanted to talk to him about Elvis."

The mention of Elvis and what is happening to a young fan, surges through the audience like an electric current. The result is high voltage outrage. They've come to the show because they were told Bruce Springsteen is the next big thing in rock and roll. And to be fair, until then, the show has been sensational. But what is he doing, they want to know? This is Memphis, home of the King. Where is the respect? All the kid wanted to do was talk to him about Elvis.

At that moment a voice is heard from the back of the auditorium, shouting, "Leave the kid alone." Charlie is small, possibly 5 feet 2 inches tall in his Cuban heel boots, so the mistake is understandable. There are more shouts from the audience of "He's only a boy" "Let him be" and "It's Little Elvis, shame on you." There are cheers when a lone Scots voice shouts: "D'ye no ken he's a wee laddie." For the first time ever, boos are heard at a Bruce Springsteen concert. The band stops playing and Springsteen walks to the front of the stage, arms outstretched, pleading to know what is going on, but there is no let-up in the catcalls and whistles. He wants to explain that it wasn't a boy, but a middle-aged man, albeit a short one, but he can't be heard above the din. Someone calls out: "Give Little Elvis a break and listen to him."

Bubba leaves his seat and dashes forward, hoping he can rescue the situation for Springsteen, and ultimately the song he's written for Elvis. The jeers change to cheers as the audience sees another young fan walk on stage. The two security men emerge from the wings, but the crowd begins to chant, "Leave the kid alone, leave the kid alone." Springsteen motions to them to back off.

Bubba says to him, "Your security guys have just manhandled Charlie Hodge, Elvis's best friend, off the stage. Not a good move, here in Memphis. All he wanted to do is tell you Elvis is interested in the song you've written for him and would like to record it. My advice is to get Charlie back on stage double quick and perform some Elvis numbers."

There are cheers and the auditorium reverberates to the noise of stamping feet as Bubba waves to the audience as he leaves the stage. The cheers are even louder when Charlie walks back on and, after a brief chat, duets with Springsteen on a medley of Elvis songs.

Springsteen and his guitar player, Steve Van Zandt, are sitting in his dressing room after the show, sipping a beer and commiserating. "Admit it, we screwed up," says The Boss.

"I can't believe it," declares Van Zandt. "We were booed. That's never happened before, but at least we turned things around by getting that little guy back on stage and doing those Elvis numbers. It got the crowd back onside."

"Yes, we did, but I still feel bad about it. The good thing is that we know that Elvis, the King, wants to record one of my songs. Do you know how much that means to me?"

Springsteen recounts the story of how, at the age of seven, he saw Elvis on TV on the Ed Sullivan Show. It was a life-changing moment; from that time all he's wanted was to be a rock and roll singer like Elvis.

He finishes his beer and says, "I know this sounds crazy, but I want to go to Graceland now. Tonight. This minute. All this has happened for a reason. It's fate, and I'm destined to meet Elvis and we're going to make great music together. It's written in the stars."

"Talking about the stars, look at the time – it's one o' clock in the morning! We can't go now."

Springsteen insists. "I hear that Elvis stays up late. He goes to bed when everybody else is getting up. There's time to see him. Come on, let's get a cab."

Van Zandt tells him: "I don't think you've thought this through, Boss. What about the song you've written for him? You haven't got it on tape to take with you."

"Don't worry. I'll write down the lyrics in the cab and go through the melody with him on one of his guitars."

The yellow cab drops them off outside the Music Gates. From where they are standing, they can see a light on in a room on the first floor of Graceland and Springsteen is convinced it's a sign that Elvis is home.

But Van Zandt is still nervous about the plan which he considers very risky. After all, it means breaking into the home of the most famous man in the world. "Listen, Boss, the place will be locked up tighter than a drum, security guards will be patrolling the grounds, and we'll be caught before we're halfway up the drive. I don't want us to spend time in the police cells downtown. It's Memphis and they'll probably throw away the key."

"I hear what you say, Steve, but I'm going in," replies Springsteen. "Even if I go alone."

"Okay, Boss. I'll stay here with the cab. While we wait for you, I'll write our names on the wall like we're regular fans."

With a boost from his guitarist, he clambers over the wall and jogs up the drive. When he gets to the house, he'll walk up to the front door, knock, and ask for Elvis: that's the plan. So far, so good: no sign of security.

As he nears the portico he stops suddenly, stunned by what he sees walking towards him: a figure that could have come from a Stephen King horror story. It's Minnie Mae, Elvis's grandmother, in a pink candlewick dressing gown, fastened at the waist by a leather belt, her hair in brown paper curlers, and green rubber boots on her feet. Most alarming of all, she's pointing a big shotgun at him.

"Ah dun seen yer, a-sneakin' up the drive," she tells him. "Now lift them hands high, but real slow like molasses on a winter's day, and reach fer the sky."

He does as she asks, while telling her that he's Bruce Springsteen, a rock and roll singer, and he's come to see Elvis.

"A singer you be a-sayin'. Well, mister, y'all look like a kidnapper ter me that's dun come ter try an' take the boy."

"No, no, no," he protests. "You've got it all wrong. I've written a song for Elvis, and he wants to record it for his new album. It's here in my pocket. Let me show you."

Minnie Mae laughs quietly to herself. "They all say that. But you ain't foolin' me none, Mr Kidnapper. Keep them hands away from yer pockets an' high in the air."

The front door opens and what could be Big Bird having a really bad day emerges and stands behind Minnie Mae. Springsteen flinches: how much weirder can it get here at Graceland?

It is, of course, Colonel Parker, shaped like an enormous acid drop on legs, in a bright yellow Hawaiian shirt, both arms tucked into slings, and black stubble on his layers of jowls. A small straw trilby is perched on the back of his head.

"I came to see what's going on," he says.

"Ah dun caught me a felon, with evil on his mind," she tells him.

Springsteen shakes his head: "No, no, no. It's not true."

"I thought Red and Sonny West were in charge of security around here," declares the Colonel. "That's why they're on the payroll. Where are they, those useless clowns? Their idea of security is making sure the doors are shut."

"Pay it no mind, Colonel. It ain't nothin' ah can't handle."

Minnie Mae moves a couple of steps nearer Springsteen, still pointing Grandpappy Hood's old buffalo gun at him. "Lissen up good, Mr Kidnapper. Ah'm a-gonna count down from ten and then ah'm a-gonna start shootin'."

She puts on her night vision goggles that she takes out of the pocket of her dressing gown. "Now ah can see real good. It's best if'n you use the time ah'm a-countin' ter skedaddle back down the drive. Ten... nine... eight..."

Springsteen is about a third of the way to the Music Gates when he hears a boom and a cloud of shotgun pellets tears through the air above his head. He's running so fast he can hardly keep his balance. As he approaches the boundary wall, he uses the Western roll technique he learned at school to leap over it and land in a heap on the other side. He's badly winded and has hurt his shoulder and knee. Ignoring any possible injuries, he scrambles up, flings himself into the yellow taxicab, followed by Van Zandt, and screams at the driver: "Go! Go! Go!"

He slams his foot on the accelerator, burns rubber and heads towards downtown. "I'm guessing you met Minnie Mae," he tells them.

The Colonel and Minnie Mae are watching the cab disappear when they are joined on the portico by Elvis, who says he thought he heard shooting. Noticing that Minnie Mae is holding a shotgun, he laughs, "Are you hunting squirrels for a fricassee?"

"No, Elvis, ah wus a-seein' a bad guy off the premises. He dun spun me some tale about him havin' a song fer yer. But he didn't fool me none, not fer one minute. Ah figured he wus gonna try an' kidnap yer."

He sighs, "That's disappointing, Dodger" – a name he sometimes calls her – "because it sounds like it was Bruce Springsteen, and it's true – he has written a song for me."

"Ah surely do declare ah'm sorry, Elvis, but it be a mighty strange time ter come a-callin' in the middle of the night about a song."

"Yes, I guess so. I hope he's not hurt."

"No, ah aimed high," she tells him. "Ah jest wanted ter give him a scare."

Elvis sighs again and shakes his head. "Ah well, it means I'm still looking for new songs for the album. I guess it's back to the drawing board."

He's about to go back indoors when he pauses, and his face brightens up. "Unless we apologise and invite him back."

"Apologise!" snorts Colonel Parker. "He broke into Graceland! And look what happened to Charlie, your gofer, when he went to his show and how he was treated. Anyway, why do you want this song?"

Elvis concedes the point but says the singer didn't know who Charlie was or what he wanted, and he quickly made amends. He adds, "I want to do his song, so I suggest we get in touch with Mr Springsteen and ask him to come back to Graceland. He must have been scared to death, so we'd better promise he won't be shot at this time."

"Ah'll cook him one of mah special down-home fricassees an' that'll make him feel real welcome," declares Minnie Mae, heading back indoors.

THE ELUSIVE HAWAIIAN-SHIRTED PIMPERNEL

"Colonel Parker, sir, there's a letter here from the Internal Revenue Service," says Bubba, his assistant. "It's addressed to you in big red capital letters and there's skull and crossbones next to the stamp. I think it must be really important."

"What letter?" he inquires, as he sits behind his desk in his office at Graceland, sifting through invoices to be paid and putting them into two piles, one which is designated as 'sometimes' and the other as 'never'.

"This one, sir, the one I am holding up in front of my face."

"I have never seen that letter and what's more, neither have you!"

"But, sir..."

"Bubba! Give me that thing that I've never seen."

Holding it between the tips of his index finger and thumb as if it were highly contagious, Colonel Parker dangles it over a wastepaper bin and sets fire to it with the end of his cigar.

"There, you see, as far as we are both concerned, if the tax people ever ask, we never saw it, it never existed."

A couple of weeks later and the Colonel is doing some overdue maintenance work to the gaming machine that he keeps in his office next to his desk. The work is necessary since he cannot recall, nor can he find a note in his diary, concerning the last time he won. He's fed up with being a serial loser and he is trying to adjust the tumbling mechanism, so that the three grinning clown faces that represent a win, will appear a lot more often.

He is like a surgeon carrying out a very delicate, painstaking operation, and he has reached a critical point in the procedure when the phone rings. Bubba isn't there to take it, so he ignores it. But it keeps on ringing, and it seems to be getting louder and more irritating and he can't concentrate on what he's doing.

"Yes!" he yells down the receiver, unable to contain his frustration at being interrupted.

"My name is Russ Russell. I'm from the Tax Evasion Investigation Unit of the Internal Revenue Service and I'd like to speak to Colonel Thomas Parker."

There is a long silence as Elvis's manager tries to recover from shock. Like a chameleon, his face changes from bright red with embarrassment to ashen white with fear.

"Am I speaking to Colonel Parker?"

"No, definitely not. Absolutely not. This is his assistant, Bubba, speaking," he replies, desperately trying to sound 40 years younger.

"We've sent him several letters in recent months, Mr Bubba, but have had no response from him. We'd like to see him urgently concerning his tax returns. In fact, 'returns' is a misnomer, since according to our records, he hasn't returned anything to the IRS for many years and there is an issue with a substantial build-up of unpaid personal taxes."

"He's away on a series of very important business meetings in New York, Las Vegas, and Hollywood on behalf of his client, Mr Elvis Presley. These negotiations can drag on and he expects to be away for a long time."

"Never mind, Mr Bubba," says the man from the IRS. "In the circumstances we will make an appointment to come to Graceland to inspect the books in his absence. Just make sure that they are available to us when we arrive, and we can then interview Colonel Parker at some later date. On that occasion he may wish to have a lawyer present, as well as his accountant. Now if we can just make a date in the diary for our visit."

"Ah, there's a problem," he answers. "You see, Colonel Parker always puts the ledgers in a Gladstone bag that he takes with him everywhere. He says he never knows when he may need to refer to them at one of his business meetings. And the office diary – he takes that with him as well."

He contrives to make a succession of buzzing and clicking noises, before banging the receiver on his desk a few times and saying he'll have to hang up.

"Look, I'm like any other good American who wants to pay his taxes," declares Colonel Parker, at a crisis meeting with Elvis and Bubba.

It is such an incredible, jaw-dropping statement that they look at each other in bewilderment, since he is not only believed to be an illegal immigrant and, therefore, not an American, but he professes to regard the imposition of taxes as an impediment to entrepreneurship and something to be avoided whenever possible. Taxes come top of the list of things that he hates to pay, followed by invoices and tips.

"The problem is that we're dealing with people who do nothing but count beans," the Colonel continues. "They latch on to hard-working businessmen like me. You see, there is a perfectly reasonable explanation, if only they were prepared to listen; I've been so busy looking after the world's greatest entertainer and America's biggest asset that, understandably, I've got a bit behind with my own tax returns."

He opens his arms in an Al Jolson-like gesture of appeal. "I'm guilty of putting Elvis first. That's where I went wrong."

He removes a grubby handkerchief from the sleeve of his jacket and blows his nose loudly, as if deeply affected by his self-sacrifice.

Bubba asks: "Shall I get you a glass of water, sir?"

"No, just let me take a moment to regain my composure," he answers, blowing his nose again while glancing furtively at Elvis who, having seen this routine several times before, is more interested in inspecting his fingernails.

Elvis wonders why his manager does not simply hand over the books so that they can be inspected, and then the IRS investigators will surely see that everything is above aboard.

He shakes his head wearily. "If only it were that simple. You see, son, they'll go through the accounts with a fine-tooth comb, looking to find a minor oversight which they'll blow up out of all proportion to show I'm somehow trying to cheat them. Then they'll follow up by hitting me with a demand for an outrageous sum in reparations. It's how they justify their miserable existence and how they stifle good old-fashioned American get-up-and-go."

Bubba raises his hand to ask a question. "What about Elvis's tax situation, sir, and your partnership with Elvis? Are they being investigated?"

There are no problems there, he assures them. "It's me they have got in their sights; it's me who has a target on his back."

Elvis is mightily relieved to hear that his affairs won't be scrutinised. "I know this might sound controversial, sir, but if there are any back taxes outstanding, why don't you just pay them?"

"There's a problem," he answers with a sigh. "I don't have the money."

"What!" exclaims Elvis, erupting like a small volcano. "That's impossible. I must have made millions of dollars this year alone from tours, seasons in Las Vegas and sales of my records. And what about all the merchandise? I don't understand! Where's all that money gone?"

He looks at Bubba and then at his manager and he knows what has happened. It has been gambled away at casinos in Las Vegas where he is always welcomed with open arms and red carpets because they know he is the world's worst gambler. And because he never wins, he keeps on playing for bigger and bigger stakes in the belief that one day he will win and recoup all his losses. But he never does. Gaming machines, poker, roulette, dice, it does not matter what he plays, he is jinxed, a Jonah.

Elvis says, with a resigned shake of his head, that just this once, in recognition of all that his manager has done for him and his career, he will lend him the money to pay his taxes.

"The trouble is, son, you don't have the money either."

This time there is a Krakatoa-scale eruption from Elvis. "What!" he bellows. He leans over the Colonel's desk, staring at him, confronting him. "What have you done with my money? Have you gambled it away as well as your own?"

"No," replies Colonel Parker, removing his handkerchief again to mop his face as he feels the heat of Elvis's anger. "None of your money has been touched. But according to my accountants, Miser & Miser, the fact is that you currently owe me about two million dollars. It's a temporary thing, a cash flow situation. But the point is, at this moment in time, you don't have the money. As much as I appreciate the offer, you can't help me."

He says what he needs is more time to find a solution to his troubles, and to do that he needs to disappear – to become invisible – so that the IRS cannot track him down before he is ready.

"I want to become like that guy in the movies – the Scarlet Pimple."

"I think you mean the Scarlet Pimpernel, sir," says Bubba helpfully.

Elvis sarcastically recites: "They seek him here, they seek him there, the IRS men seek him everywhere, the elusive Hawaiian-shirted Pimpernel."

Angry though he is, he doesn't want to abandon his manager to the wolves, and it is he who comes up with a possible hiding place – the long-mothballed nuclear bunker that Colonel Parker insisted on building at Graceland during the Cuban missile crisis when he feared that the Russians might bomb Memphis.

After some modifications have been made to equip it as an emergency office for the Colonel while he hides there, it is decided to stage a trial run.

When an unidentified car is seen driving through the Music Gates an air raid klaxon sounds its warning which can be heard blaring out all over Graceland. This is the signal for Colonel Parker to immediately leave his office and head for the hall where Elvis, accompanied by Bubba and Charlie Hodge, his old friend and chief gofer, is standing near the entrance to the bunker with a stopwatch.

By the time Colonel Parker reaches the hall he has built up his speed to a slow trot of about 5 mph, causing him to wheeze like a broken accordion. He bangs his hand against a button on the wall and the carpet automatically rolls back and a trapdoor in the floor opens. The Colonel heads down the steps, pushing another button on his way down which closes the trapdoor and automatically slides the carpet back in place.

At that moment the front doorbell rings. He's made good his escape, but only just.

Not bad, considers Elvis, as he shows the stopwatch to Bubba and Charlie. "Luckily it was a test run, but to be on the safe side, he needs to shave another five seconds off his time," he suggests. "And I can still hear him down there gasping for breath. What can we do to get him up to speed and in better shape?"

Bubba sighs. "All things considered, it's probably too late."

It takes no more than three days before everybody at Graceland is utterly fed up with the bunker hideaway plan. It is making their lives hell.

Quite a few unidentified cars and trucks turn up each day, and because the Colonel doesn't want to take a chance that the IRS men might be concealed in one of them, the klaxon is constantly booming out over Graceland.

Colonel Parker has made the 'dash' so many times from his office to the bunker that his times are getting slower, not faster, as he becomes increasingly exhausted.

"I declare my nerves are in shreds," complains Priscilla. "What with that klaxon and Colonel Parker clumping through the house like a geriatric elephant I've got a permanent headache."

She cites the occasion when she was taken by surprise while doing her eye makeup, and that can take a long time building up the layers. The sudden noise of the klaxon made her jump, and she ended up with mascara smeared across her face. "I looked like a circus clown," she sulks.

Charlie says that he is always clearing up after Scatter, Elvis's pet chimpanzee, because all the commotion has given him the squitters.

The bunker plan is put to a vote and every single person in Graceland, including Colonel Parker, votes in favour of abandoning it. "I haven't got time to think of an answer for the IRS people because I'm spending all my time running backwards and forwards and falling asleep through exhaustion," he says.

The next idea involves a visit from the top makeup people sent by Hal Wallis, the producer of nine of Elvis's movies, in the search for a convincing disguise that will allow the Colonel to move around Graceland without being recognised by a visitor.

The makeup team ask Colonel Parker to stand still as if he is posing for a portrait while they circle around him, considering the options, and stroking chins. Since he is reputed to be the third fattest man in America it is a small field of possibilities. Someone suggests Orson Welles, but it does not find much favour: he's too thin to pass for the Colonel.

The answer they come up with, bearing in mind his body shape and jowls, is Alfred Hitchcock.

It must be said that there is a certain similarity between them; a little work on his hair, a shave, putting him in a dark suit, white shirt and tie and getting him to keep practising sticking out his lower lip and – hey presto! – someone who looks like an overweight Alfred Hitchcock.

Meanwhile the IRS Tax Evasion Investigation Unit has decided that the time has come to get tough with someone they are convinced is an inveterate tax dodger on a grand scale. A court order is issued, requiring him to hand over his books; failure to do so could result in a substantial fine and a term of imprisonment.

They feel that it will be good for the US government to recover all the monies he owes, as well as being a boost for the reputation of the unit in catching such a big fish ("a whale would be more appropriate," suggests a minion to guffaws around the office).

The IRS spy on the ground with the binoculars outside the Music Gates, who has been watching the comings and goings at Graceland, reports that he has seen Alfred Hitchcock moving around inside the house. But no sign of the Colonel.

"Perhaps Hitchcock's in on it, too?" suggests one of the team.

The spy adds that he's been told by fans who congregate outside the gates that Liberace was seen recently driving up to the house.

"Let's make a note on the file," says Russ Russell, their leader. "We might just be on the verge of breaking up a secret cell of big-name tax dodgers."

The Big Day finally arrives and every member of the IRS Tax Evasion Investigation Unit crowds around the desk to watch the opening of the package that contains Colonel Parker's books. Finally, they will be able to begin a forensic examination to search for what they believe are the missing millions of dollars in unpaid taxes.

Russ Russell points out that Elvis, the world's greatest entertainer and the King of Rock and Roll, must make millions every year from his shows, records, movies, and merchandise. His manager has a contract that gives him a 50 per cent share of the King's earnings. "Just imagine how much he must be raking in," he says.

"If we can nail this guy then it will send out a message that nobody will escape, that we will hunt them down relentlessly, no matter who they are and how big a name and recover every single dollar that they have tried to conceal."

He opens the parcel to gasps of astonishment and cries of "I don't believe it!" as if they have unlocked a Pandora's box of horrors. Then comes complete silence; the shock and awe has caused everyone to hold their breath.

They are looking at two books by the famous TV chef Julia Child, *Mastering the Art of French Cooking* and *The French Chef Cookbook*.

"Let's check with the delivery company," says someone finally breaking the silence. "Obviously, there's been a mistake somewhere down the line."

"There's no mistake. Can't you see what's going on here?" the chief says to his team. They shake their heads.

"Look again! There are two cookbooks because he's sending us a message. He's telling us 'I'm cooking the books and laughing at you'. Oh boy, I'm going to nail that slippery Colonel Parker if it's the last thing I do. First, get me that assistant of his on the phone."

"Hello, this is Colonel Parker's assistant, Bubba, speaking. How can I help you?"

"This is Russ Russell, the head of the Tax Evasion Investigation Unit of the Internal Revenue Service. We've spoken before."

"Have we?" says Bubba, baffled. He certainly has no memory of it.

"I don't suppose Colonel Parker is there?"

"No sir, the last I heard he was in Hollywood... or was it the Catskills? I'm not sure."

"Let me explain, Mr Bubba. We were expecting a delivery of Colonel Parker's accounts books because we need to investigate if there are any unpaid taxes due to the Internal Revenue Service. However, what we've received are two cookbooks. Can you shed any light on this?"

"I'm sorry to hear that, sir. I believe that those books should have been delivered to Mrs Parker. I'm told she's an excellent cook."

"If I'm correct, Mr Bubba, then she should have received Colonel Parker's ledgers, so we'll arrange to collect them from her. Please give me her home address."

"There's a problem, because she's left to join Colonel Parker in Hollywood... or is it the Catskills?"

"Let me make this crystal clear, Mr Bubba. We will find those books and if there are any unpaid taxes due, we will recover every single cent and almost certainly impose a severe financial penalty, together with a term of imprisonment. We'll be in touch."

A few days later, a fleet of vans pulls up outside the portico at Graceland and out pile 16 members of the IRS's Tax Evasion Investigation Unit, each one clutching a clipboard, led by their chief, Russ Russell. As they begin to climb the steps Minnie Mae emerges from the front door, cocking Grandpappy Hood's old buffalo gun.

She tells them: "Y'all should stop right there an' don't breathe cus the slightest movement might jest cause mah trigger finger ter twitch."

Russ Russell waves a piece of paper at her and says: "We have a warrant..."

Boom! Minnie Mae blasts a hole in the side of one of the vans. Russ and his men run back down the steps and gather in a huddle near the wrecked van. The hole is so big that, with very little work, it could be converted into a mobile burger van.

"D'ya all see wut jest happened? Didn't ah say don't make a move? Like fools, yer didn't listen to me." She shakes her head sorrowfully. "An' ah still got me one shot left, boys, if'n you wanna try yer luck."

Elvis dashes out on to the portico and wraps his arms around his grandmother. "This is a disgrace," he yells at the IRS men. "How dare you turn up mob-handed and frighten a frail old lady!"

He shepherds her inside the house, saying that he'll take care of things from here. Russ Russell shows Elvis the order empowering them to search Graceland. "Is Colonel Parker here?" he asks.

Elvis shakes his head.

It takes the IRS squad two days to search every room in the mansion; they find no sign of the missing books that detail the Colonel's financial affairs. Nor do they find Colonel Parker; one man, however, says he caught a glimpse of Alfred Hitchcock in the hall, but then he seemed to vanish without trace.

As they are about to climb into their vans to head back to Washington, Elvis reminds them that they ought to inspect his cars, motorbikes and jets parked on the far side of Graceland, since the missing books might be hidden there. They should leave no stone unturned, he says.

There is a collective groan when the IRS guys learn that there are more than 20 cars, 12 motorbikes and 2 jets to be searched. Another two days are wasted in finding nothing at all, not even a cigarette stub, because all the ashtrays are spotlessly clean thanks to Charlie's diligence as a cleaner.

Russ Russell cannot hide his disappointment when he announces that they are about to leave Graceland empty-handed.

There is a sharp intake of breath from Elvis. "Is that wise, Russ?" he inquires. "Have you eliminated every possibility?"

"I think so," he replies nervously, wondering what he might be about to suggest.

"Here at Graceland Colonel Parker is known as 'Secret Squirrel' because of his habit of burying things in the ground all over Graceland. And I'm sure it's not nuts that he's hiding. I'm betting that somewhere out there is a hastily dug hole that could conceal his books." He winks and taps the side of his nose with his forefinger. "Don't say I told you!"

There are 19 acres of grounds and another three days go by without finding what they are looking for. The IRS guys have now been at Graceland for a week.

"While you were out there did you remember to inspect the stables?" asks Elvis.

"No," responds Russ, looking crushed and dearly wanting to leave Graceland as soon as possible.

"Naturally, you'll have to muck out the stables first to do a thorough inspection," declares Elvis. "Then there's my dog Old Shep's kennel, although I should warn you that he's got fleas and doesn't smell too good. I think you can forget searching my pet chimpanzee Scatter's accommodation. He and Colonel Parker don't like each other so the Colonel is unlikely to stash his books there. But come to think of it – that might make it the ideal place, like a double bluff."

Since arriving at Graceland, it feels as if the IRS men have entered one of the innermost circles of hell. The team has gathered expectantly by the vans, hoping they'll be finally heading home. When Russ breaks the news that there's more to do there are dark looks, groans and swear words that hint a rebellion might not be far away. Another day is spent without finding the Colonel's accounts and leaving their Brooks Brothers suits stained and smelling whiffy.

Everyone at Graceland gathers on the portico to wave goodbye to the guys from the IRS Tax Evasion Investigation Unit. As they drive down the drive towards the Music Gates, one of them looks back towards the house. "Just a minute!" he exclaims. "It might be a trick of the eye, but is that Alfred Hitchcock standing at the back and waving?"

"I don't care!" shouts Russ, their leader. "Just get me out of here. Keep driving and step on the gas."

It has been 24 hours since the IRS men left and Elvis and Priscilla are enjoying a ride in the grounds of Graceland; he is on his favourite horse, a golden palomino called Rising Sun, while she is riding Domino, a black Tennessee walking horse that Elvis bought for her. After a gallop they pull up to give the horses a rest. They dismount to walk, holding the reins of their horses.

"Did you know that Colonel Parker came to see me privately?" says Priscilla.

"No, I didn't," replies Elvis, looking surprised. Relations between them are frosty at best.

She continues: "He probably thought I was going to get you to sack him over this investigation into unpaid taxes. But he swore to me that the IRS people have got it all wrong and he will prove his innocence. He just needs a bit more time. Things got temporarily overlooked because he's been so busy looking after you and me."

"You?"

"Yes, me. I was surprised, too. He's arranged for me to appear as the main feature in the next edition of Vogue in a piece along the lines of 'Queen of Rock and Roll at home in her palace'. They're going to send a top writer; he mentioned Truman Capote or Gore Vidal. And Cecil Beaton is coming over from England to take the pictures. He always takes the photos for Her Majesty the Queen, you know, so I bet she's given him permission to come. It's very kind of her; I'll send her a thank-you letter."

"And send her a copy of the magazine when it comes out," adds Elvis.

"In the circumstances, I think I have a responsibility to you and Graceland to agree to do this feature with Vogue. The whole thing resonates exquisite taste and class, which is how I want our home to appear to our friends and your fans. For the time being then, Elvis, I think we should give Colonel Parker the chance to sort things out."

Elvis nods his head to signify his agreement. They remount and trot back to the stables where Charlie Hodge is waiting to rub down the horses and feed them.

It is the day the men in the Tax Evasion Investigation Unit at the IRS have long dreamt about – the arrival of a parcel containing the books of Colonel Parker's financial accounts. Russ Russell pauses after the first ceremonial snip of the scissors to bask in the cheers from the rest of the team. Thousands of hours have been devoted to get to the point where they can investigate the books and discover how many millions of dollars he must owe in back taxes. It is a major victory for the department: sightings of Bigfoot are more common than the appearance of his tax returns.

He peels back the paper to reveal two suspiciously pristine-looking ledgers and a covering letter from the Colonel's accountants, Miser & Miser, claiming that the accounts reveal he is owed more than $2 million in overpaid taxes. "Our client would welcome immediate remuneration," they state.

He is too stunned to speak and hands over the letter for the others to read.

When he subsequently goes to see the head of the Internal Revenue Service, he is told that the decision has been made right at the very top that the money should be paid to Colonel Parker.

"Surely, sir, that's not possible," protests Russ. "This man is a tax dodger on an industrial scale. There are people in my department who were still in kindergarten the last time he submitted a return, and that was when he was running a dancing chickens act. Even then there was a dispute over his claims concerning the cost of seed corn and hay."

"I'm truly sorry for you, Russ, and your team in the Tax Evasion Investigation Unit. But you must be realistic. You clocked up thousands of hours and the result is that IRS ends up having to pay him more than two million dollars.

"You took on the guy who manages Elvis, a national treasure, the world's greatest entertainer, and a man with millions of fans, including President Nixon and his family. Elvis might, understandably, have got very upset about this – and nobody wants to cross Elvis." He beckons Russ to come closer and he whispers, "Not even the Oval Office."

Russ's boss tells him that there is a question mark over the future of the whole department. The consensus is that they should be given one more chance, but they cannot afford another failure. They need to deliver a big name on a platter, together with the recovery of a substantial sum in unpaid taxes, to rebuild their reputation and guarantee their future.

Back in the office Russ calls the team together to inform that he was reprimanded over the Colonel Parker case. He and Elvis have friends in the very highest places.

He bangs his fist on his desk and shouts: "The truth is we were right, and he's got away with it. But we've been given another chance and this time we're gonna nail the guy we target."

They all look at each other, wondering who it could be.

"Okay, team, I've decided: we're going after Alfred Hitchcock. We've seen with our own eyes that he's a regular visitor to Graceland and I'm betting he's in the same big-name tax-dodging syndicate as Colonel Parker. Getting Hitchcock might well give us the information we need to net Liberace and the spider in the centre of the web, Colonel Parker."

Colonel Parker is happily back at Graceland, confident that the crisis over the investigation into his tax affairs is an unpleasant, distant memory. Yes, it was 'a close-run thing' but he took care of business and fooled the IRS investigators. Affable is how he feels as he sits in his office with Elvis and Bubba, puffing away on one of his finest Walmart cigars, specially selected for the occasion.

"Whatever happened to your original set of books, Colonel, sir, the ones you used to keep locked in your desk?" asks his assistant. "The IRS men spent days searching high and low, but they never found them. They must have been very well hidden."

The Colonel laughs so heartily that ash is shaken from the end of his cigar and spills down the front of his new nuclear orange Hawaiian shirt. There is a sizzle as a small hole is burnt by a hot piece of ash.

"Hide in plain sight, that's the secret," he beams. "Come with me and I'll show you."

He leads them to the Jungle Room and stands next to a bookcase. "Now tell me what you see."

Elvis and Bubba bend down to run their eyes along each shelf. They repeat the process but admit they can see nothing amiss.

"Exactly," declares the Colonel. "And neither did the IRS."

He removes a couple of books and tells them: "Here they are." He

is so proud of himself. In a lifetime of cons, going right back to his days in carny, this must be one of his very best. If there were ever to be a Fifth Horseman of the Apocalypse, it would be Colonel Parker and his cons.

Elvis and Bubba find themselves looking at 'Grim Fairy Tales Volumes One and Two'.

"These are my priceless set of accounts with their new titles. D'yer get it?"

"Oh, yes, I get it!" Elvis laughs loudly. "I bet these figures make amazing fairy tales and they'll be grim reading, too." He walks over to his manager, slaps him on the back and shakes his hand.

Then his expression quickly changes from amusement to seriousness. "But grim reading for who? That's the question, isn't it?"

There is a look of bemusement on the Colonel's face as he tries to withdraw his hand, but Elvis grips it more tightly.

"I like a good read before I go to sleep, and I'm sure I'll enjoy these fairy tales. And these new accountants I'm talking to – they're great readers too."

'New accountants' are words that cause fear to run through him like an electric current. "Ho, ho, ho," he laughs like a jolly Father Christmas, trying to lighten the darkening atmosphere.

Still gripping his hand Elvis suggests they return to his office for a chat about their partnership agreement.

"This two million dollars that you're receiving from the IRS for overpaid taxes – that's not a fairy tale, is it?" questions Elvis.

"Er... no," replies his manager, now back behind his desk. He pulls out an old handkerchief from the sleeve of his jacket to mop his face which has assumed the shape and colour of a plum tomato with whiskers.

"Now our contract says that we split the money we earn fifty-fifty, so by my reckoning, half of that money should be coming to me. What do you say?"

"Er..." is all that he's able to offer. The Colonel is caught on the hop and for the time being, the best that the author or 'Grim Fairy Tales' can offer is a grimace.

THE RETURN OF MAE WEST

Elvis is strolling through the lobby of the International Hotel in Las Vegas, having just finished a rehearsal with his band and backing singers in preparation for tonight's show. He has a towel around his neck which he's using to mop his face. With him is Charlie Hodge, his old friend and gofer-in-chief, who is carrying a thermos flask of iced water in one hand and some plastic cups in the other, ever ready to be of service.

Elvis pauses, as if something has just occurred to him, and veers off towards the reception desk to check if there are any messages for him.

As he talks to the clerk, he notices his expression suddenly change. He looks shocked and Elvis is aware of an instant hubbub of gasps and chatter behind him; he turns to see what's going on.

Walking towards him, hips swaying metronomically from side to side like a pendulum, is Mae West. How can anyone walk like that without falling over, he thinks? Although it's early afternoon she's dressed in a low-cut shiny, silver gown that reflects the lights like a mirror ball and fits her as if she'd been wrapped in tinfoil. Elvis is mesmerised.

Following her are her three maids, dressed in traditional French maid outfits, each one pulling a large trunk case – one for her gowns, one for her hats, and one for her jewellery and make-up.

Mae West shimmies up to Elvis, removes a long cigarette holder from her mouth, and pouts. "Hello again, big boy," she says, patting her platinum blond hair and fluttering her eyelashes, heavily weighted with mascara. Elvis mumbles 'hello' and dabs his face with his towel. He's starting to heat up and turn red.

He's had a run-in with her in the past when, by mistake, she was cast as Jane in a Tarzan film he was making, and it took a lot of effort to get rid of her. As part of the deal, he agreed to make an album with her. He was deeply seared by the whole experience. (See 'You Tarzan and Me Jane' in Elvis: The Siege of Graceland and Other Stories.)

Mae West turns to look at Charlie. "Who's the little guy? Is that a cocktail shaker he's holding? I know it's a bit early in the day, but I could sure use a dry martini and a stuffed olive. Can you fix that, little guy?"

Charlie nervously backs away and tries to hide himself behind Elvis.

"He doesn't say much, does he? What is he – your personal dumb waiter?"

"What brings you here, Miss West?" asks Elvis.

"You mean apart from wanting to see you and restore the sizzle in our friendship? Haven't you heard, my little chickadee? Haven't you seen all the publicity? I'm front-page news. I'm here for the annual Mae West convention that's being held here at the International. My fans insist on doing it every year and making a big fuss of me."

There's a sudden, sharp intake of breath and she looks horrified; she puts a hand over her mouth, but not so close that it will smudge her lipstick. "Oh no, I've just realised," she gasps. "I hope my convention won't affect the attendance at your shows, Elvis."

"No need to worry, Miss West," he replies. "All the shows are sold out."

"Ah yes, but will all those seats be filled? What will happen when they learn I'm here being interviewed on stage and answering questions from my fans? I'll be signing books, running an auction of memorabilia, doing some cabaret, and showing my films. Sorry, Elvis, but I'm predicting an exodus. And by the way, did I mention that Cary Grant will be here?"

"Cary Grant!" declares Elvis, his surprise causing his eyebrows to soar like kites up into the sky. "The Cary Grant?"

"Yes, he comes to every convention. He's always so grateful to me. I taught him everything he knows." She looks archly at Elvis, and adds, "And about acting, too."

One of her maids bustles over to put a new cigarette in Mae West's holder and hold up a mirror so she can check her appearance.

The desk clerk starts coughing. "Excuse me, Miss West, but there's some information I need so I can complete your registration. I've not been able to find out, so can you please tell me, the year you were born."

"It's 1935," she answers.

"Hey, that's the same year as me!" comments Elvis.

The desk clerk coughs again. "I'm so sorry, Miss West, but did I hear you correctly? This information is supposed to be accurate."

She glares at him. "I should know! Put down 1934 and see if that sounds any better!"

"Thank you, Miss West. You're in the Frank Sinatra Suite."

Elvis looks puzzled, and remarks that he always stays there when he's performing at the International.

"Yea, that's right, King," pipes up Charlie, ever the loyal ally.

The desk clerk flicks through the register of bookings. "That's usually the case, Mr Presley – and I don't know how this has happened – but Miss West is definitely booked in at the Frank Sinatra suite."

"Now you know where I am, and it sounds to me like you know your way there, so why don't you come up and see me sometime?" she says to Elvis, winking at him. She waves her diamond and platinum wristwatch in front of his face and tells him: "Do you know why men always give me expensive Swiss watches? Because I'm a girl who likes a good time. And I see it's also time for me to go and get ready for my champagne reception. Will you be coming?"

She blows a small puff of cigarette smoke into his face and sashays towards the elevators, followed by her maids dragging her cases. Elvis can't take his eyes off the hypnotic motion of her hips. "Elvis!" shouts Charlie, tugging at the sleeve of his jumpsuit, trying to break the spell.

Earlier, when Elvis left to go to rehearsals, Colonel Parker, his manager, finds himself irresistibly drawn to the casino. Although it's only been a few months since Elvis's last season of shows at the International, he's anxious to find out if there's anything different. Are there any new games? Have the gaming tables been rearranged in the room? Are there more one-armed bandits? Is there a new carpet? There is so much to discover; he can feel a tingle of excitement running through his body like electricity, right down to his fingertips. Like a hippopotamus sensing the nearby presence of a river, his pace increases to a trot, such is his eagerness to start playing.

He pauses at the very first gaming machine he comes to, drops a chip into the slot, pulls the lever – and loses. *Oh well*, he thinks to himself, *I'm sure it's not a bad omen. I've got a good feeling about today.*

Unfortunately, Colonel Parker is the unluckiest gambler in the world, and he's on a losing streak longer than the Mississippi. If he were to bet on two flies climbing up a windowpane, it's the Colonel's fly that would fall down, lie on its back, and die. He's also the dumbest gambler in the world – the only man on Planet Earth to bet against Secretariat completing the Triple Crown in 1973 by winning the Belmont Stakes, after already coming first in the Kentucky Derby and the Preakness Stakes. Secretariat won the Belmont by a record distance of 31 lengths and in record time. The Colonel's horse finished last.

He wanders around the casino as if it were a buffet, serving himself to large helpings of blackjack, roulette, poker, and craps, before returning to the gaming machines. He loses at each halt on his journey, but he's always prepared to move on to the next game, convinced his luck will change. How can he lose when his jacket pocket is stuffed full of lucky charms, including a mangy rabbit's foot, a piece of paper from a fortune cookie, and an old ace of spades playing card?

In two hours, he's used up the entire $250,000 loaned to him by the International against the profits to be earned from Elvis's shows. He decides to go and see Salvatore, the general manager, to ask for a top-up of, say, another $250,000. That should keep him going for a couple of days until his big win comes along. He softly sings *The Man Who Broke the Bank at Monte Carlo* as he goes up in the elevator.

Salvatore's office has a floor-to-ceiling wall of glass that overlooks the casino; he's dressed in an evening suit and black bow tie, as if he's ready to leave for dinner at any moment. He gets up to greet Colonel Parker and shake his hand. He is, after all, their best client, the man who almost single-handedly bankrolls the business as a result of the money the hotel makes from Elvis's shows, coupled with the Colonel's enormous gambling losses.

"I'm always delighted to see you, Colonel. Thanks for dropping in. I noticed you working your way around the casino, so tell me, how did you get on? A big win? Do I need to take out my chequebook?" *That'll be the day*, he chuckles to himself. His slides the silver box on his desk that contains his specially imported Havana cigars towards the Colonel who takes one out, which he lights, and pops another two in the top pocket of his jacket.

Colonel Parker shakes his head and looks sorrowful. "I've been very unlucky, Sal. Lady Luck didn't smile at me today."

"Never mind, there's always tomorrow."

"But that's the point, Sal, there won't be a tomorrow. I've used up all of that loan."

"What!" Sal erupts. "All two hundred and fifty thousand dollars in just two hours!"

"Several times I was oh so close to a big win. I knew I was being mocked by Lady Luck; she was taunting me, and I wasn't going to stand for it, so I kept going. Then before I knew it the money had gone. But I believe I've got her on the run. I just need another two hundred and fifty thousand dollars to tide me over for a couple of days."

Now it's Sal's turn to look sorrowful. "Colonel, it's not like the old days." He wrings his hands to illustrate his distress. "I'm dealing with a new board of directors who are all bean-counters from Wall Street. We're in the entertainment business, me and you, but with these guys, having a club soda and reading a spreadsheet is their idea of having a good time. I used up a lot of goodwill extracting that quarter of a million dollars. There's no way they're going to sanction another dime.

"But, hey, why don't you do what you always do, and add on another couple of shows to Elvis's season? That way everybody's happy, maybe apart from Elvis, and your slate gets wiped clean."

"There's a problem, Sal. This time I can't add on any more shows. Elvis is committed to leaving immediately after the last show to go on holiday to Hawaii with Priscilla and Lisa Marie. I'd rather not have to face Priscilla if it gets cancelled."

"Given your financial situation, Colonel," says Sal, "I'd say it's worth asking Elvis to see if the holiday could be delayed for just a couple of days. After all, he's agreed before to do extra shows."

He is beginning to feel very queasy, and it's not due to the expensive cigar he's smoking instead of one of his usual Walmart two-for-the-price-of-one specials. He might well be able to persuade Elvis to talk to Priscilla about the postponement, but at some point, he knows he'll have to face the fury of the Tiny Terror.

Urged on by his manager, Elvis rings home to speak to his wife and after the usual pleasantries, he mumbles his way through asking if they can delay their family holiday to Hawaii.

"I'm not sure I heard that right," comments Priscilla. "Would you mind saying it again."

He informs her that by popular request, he has been asked to extend his Las Vegas season by a couple of nights.

"Elvis, you can stop right there. There aren't going to be any extra dates. Once your contract is done, you, me, and Lisa Marie are flying directly from Las Vegas to Hawaii. We've earned this long vacation so we can spend time together as a family. The answer, therefore, is no."

"But, honey sugar, just two extra shows and we can still have a great holiday together."

"Elvis, enough! I know exactly what's behind this. Because it's happened before. Your manager – I can't bring myself to speak his name – has been gambling again and, as usual, he's lost. He's up to his old tricks. He wants to pay back the money he owes by getting you to do extra shows. But not this time, oh no, and never again!"

Priscilla tells him that she will be flying on the next plane from Memphis to Las Vegas to make sure that nothing happens to spoil their holiday plans. "I want to be there on the spot in case there's any more of this nonsense. Are you staying in the Frank Sinatra suite as usual?" she inquires.

There is a silence at the other end of the line, before Elvis mutters, "Er, no…"

"Whaddya mean 'no'? You always stay there. It's the best suite in the hotel and you're their biggest star. Where the hell are you?"

"I'm in the Dean Martin suite."

"I don't believe it! Are they trying to insult you? Tell me, then, who's staying in the Frank Sinatra suite who's a bigger star than you?"

"It's Mae West."

At the other end of the line Elvis hears a stream of expletives that he's never heard Priscilla utter before. He's shocked she even knew them. "Mae West! That gold digger! Remember her in that Tarzan film you made! She's always trying to get her claws into you. Elvis, I'm on my way. For the next few hours stay away from Mae West and that wretch who's supposed to be your manager. Do absolutely nothing till I get there. Got it?"

"Sure thing, honey sugar. Got it. Do nothing."

Mae West is sitting, feet up, on a chaise longue in the Frank Sinatra suite, cigarette holder in one hand, while the other one hovers over a box of chocolates.

There's a loud, rapid knocking on the door.

"Hmm, I wonder who that can be?" she says. "I like my men to be keen, but not desperate." She looks across at Colonel Parker. "Our meeting is supposed to be confidential, Colonel. Best make yourself scarce."

He decides to hide behind the curtains where he'll be able to hear what's going on. After all, you never know what you might learn that might be to your advantage.

"Is that you again, Elvis, you naughty boy?" Mae West calls out. "Luckily for you, I've been resting."

The knocking becomes louder and more urgent. She signals with her eyes to a maid to answer the door.

Priscilla bursts into the room like a champagne cork from a bottle, looking this way and that, and demanding to know where's Elvis.

Mae West taps ash from her cigarette holder and looks around the room in a leisurely manner. "Well, he sure isn't here, honey. And may I ask who you are, interrupting my rest and recuperation?"

"I'm Mrs Priscilla Presley, his wife."

"Well, honey, it seems a little careless of you to lose your husband, but if it were me, the first place I'd look is in his suite."

"I did and he wasn't there. And when I knocked, it sounded like you were expecting him. I demand to know where he is and what's going on!"

"Me, too!"

Priscilla, still suspicious, walks further into the room and slowly looks around. At the far end she notices a bulge the size of a large pillow protruding from the curtains and, peeping out from beneath, the toes of a pair of shoes. She strides over and flings them open.

"You!" she declares, seeing Colonel Parker standing there. "What are you doing skulking behind the curtains."

"No, you misunderstand, Priscilla. I was just making sure this window was firmly closed. We could feel a terrible draught in here. But I think I've sorted it out now."

She glares at him and jabs a long red fingernail into his Hawaiian shirt. "You don't fool me. You were hiding. What are you two cooking up?"

She turns to face Mae West and declares: "Whatever it is, if it involves Elvis or postponing our holiday, you can forget it!"

"Ho ho ho," laughs Colonel Parker, like a Santa Claus handing out presents. "Obviously, Miss West and I have a mutual interest in show business, and we were just swapping notes. It always pays to keep your finger on the pulse of what's going on. Isn't that right, Miss West?"

She pats her hair, shrugs, and says, "Sure."

There's a tapping on the door; when one of the maids goes to answer it, Priscilla signals for her to stay where she is, telling her: "Leave this to me!"

She flings open the door and shouts "Gotcha!" before stammering: "S-s-sorry, Mr G-G-Grant. I didn't realise it was you."

"By Jove! May I ask who you are, scaring me like that?" says a puzzled-looking Cary Grant; he's dressed in a beautifully tailored double-breasted grey suit, waistcoat, and spats, and is holding a silver-topped cane with which he knocked on the door.

"I'm Priscilla Presley. I'm married to Elvis. I thought it was him at the door – but it was you. I'm so sorry."

"Ah, yes, Elvis, the rock and roll entertainer. I say, do you mind awfully if I come in?"

Cary Grant walks in, nods to Mae West, and says he's come to talk through what they're going to do at the convention. He notices Colonel Parker and inquiries, "And who is this portly gentleman who looks like W C Fields?"

"I'm Colonel Parker, the manager of Elvis Presley, Hollywood's highest earning actor and the star of thirty-one movies, every one of which made money," he responds with a glare. He can do cheap shots as well and smirks as he asks, "What movie are you working on at the moment?"

Cary Grant rubs his chin as if deep in thought. "Hmm, that's a lot of movies your boy has made. But I don't remember any of them."

Mae West tells them: "Now, now, behave, boys! I think we'd better have a drink and relax." She beckons to one of her maids and requests her to fix some martinis, and to make them very dry. "Tension causes wrinkles and I spend a lot of time and dollars avoiding them, so please help me out."

After consulting his watch, Cary Grant announces that the sun is over the yardarm. "Excellent idea," he concurs.

They hear a rat-tat-tat on the door. They are all sitting comfortably, the martinis are working their magic, and the atmosphere is much improved. When the knocks are repeated, they joke among themselves as to who it might be.

"It looks like it's going to get frightfully crowded in here, Mae," laughs Cary Grant. "Has there been a change of plan and you're going to hold the convention in your suite?"

When one of the maids opens the door, Elvis hurries in, saying, "Mae, can I have a word?" The rest of what he was going to say dies in his mouth as he looks around the room. Even after all those films in which he's acted, he cannot disguise his surprise. Following him is Charlie Hodge, his faithful gofer.

"Hey, Priscilla, we've found your husband," quips Mae West. "And he's brought his dumb waiter with him."

"Tell me, Elvis, what was the word you wanted to have with Mae West?" says Priscilla, eyeing him suspiciously.

With Elvis struggling to think of something, Mae West decides to come to his rescue. "He's come to tell me that, in spite of all the money he's being offered, he's determined to go on holiday with you and your daughter."

"That's right," he declares, with the merest hint of a nod to Mae.

"Excellent!" exclaims Priscilla, and by way of celebration, she requests another martini.

Later, when all the others have left, Mae West and Colonel Parker resume discussing the $350,000 loan she is going to give him so that he can repay Salvatore at the International, as well as having enough cash to cover his expenses over the next few days.

"What about the interest?" he asks.

"Colonel, I'm always interested in my money."

"I mean I was thinking of maybe an interest rate of one or two per cent."

She grips her long cigarette holder as if it were a brush and she was about to add a dab of paint to a portrait. "That's a very funny joke, Colonel," she says. "Did you ever work in comedy?"

She continues: "I normally charge forty per cent interest – the Colonel's face goes white – but for an old pal who's also kinda cute, I'll do a special rate of fifteen per cent."

Colonel Parker tries hard to quell his palpitations and put on a brave face. "You think I'm cute, do you? I don't think even Mrs Parker would say I'm cute."

"Yes, but in the way that some people thought King Kong was cuter than Fay Wray." She pauses while a maid fits a new cigarette in her holder. "Did you know they offered me that part? I turned it down, of course. I was working with Cary Grant on *I'm No Angel*, which was much more to my taste in all sorts of interesting ways." She smirks and pats her hair.

"I told them, 'Give it to Fay Wray. She deserves a break.' There were so many people in Hollywood then and now – actors and actresses, technicians, set builders – struggling to get by. I was pleased to help the kid."

"Mae, you've got a heart of gold. That being the case, I wonder if you might reconsider that interest rate of fifteen per cent to help a businessman such as myself in these difficult times."

"You're so funny. You crack me up." She carries on smoking, saying nothing for a minute, although it seems much longer to the Colonel, expectantly awaiting her answer.

"There's something my fans have been urging me to do for a long time," she finally says.

"Not retire, surely." He keeps a straight face but is pleased with his jibe.

When she tells him, he sighs deeply like a walrus that has missed out on his fish supper. "Doing a film or a show with Elvis – I reckon that's nigh on impossible."

"I thought so. But it's the dream of all my fans and, if by any chance, it was to come true, then it would make the interest rate disappear. And if I was really impressed, I might even agree to a cut in how much you owe me."

As the third fattest man in America Colonel Parker is never going to be able to dance a jig as he makes his way into the casino at the International, having just repaid $250,000 to Salvatore, who looked distinctly peeved at getting his money back. *On the Sunny Side of the Street*, which he hums to himself, reflects his optimism of how well things are going.

As far as Salvatore is concerned, Colonel Parker was a banker to lose the money with the usual result that more Elvis shows would be added to the season at a discounted rate. He'd hinted as much to the board of directors. They won't be happy. A searing pain in his stomach tells him the bad news has reached his ulcer. "That's all I need," he moans, as he starts to munch a mouthful of tablets.

Walking through the casino, Colonel Parker suddenly stops, his attention taken by a strange, unworldly sight. Over in the corner a roulette table is bathed in a single beam of bright light from above; he likens it to a spotlight that's trained on Elvis when he performs. A siren voice seems to coo, 'Colonel, come to me'. It must be a sign that destiny and his longed-for big win awaits him. The croupier notices him looking and smiles. Everything is right. Can it be that Lady Luck has finally decided to embrace him? He knows what he must do.

He counts his steps as he walks towards the roulette table: 33. That must be his lucky number. He decides to make a small investment from the loan that Mae West has given him: $5,000 on No. 33. He loses. Did he miscount the number of steps? He bets on No. 32 and loses again.

He cannot understand it, so he returns to where he was standing when he first saw the roulette table in the beam of light and recounts his steps: 34. That must be the answer and he doubles his stake. And loses again. He decides to try a different tack and bets on 7, the number of letters in Mae West's name. Same result.

No matter what he tries, he loses every time, before finally deciding to give up after losing $50,000. What to do? He can't go back to Mae West, having only just been given the money less than an hour ago. Perhaps he can go and see Salvatore, the general manager of the International. After all, he was, for him, very quick to repay that $250,000 loan. He knows it'll need to be a pretty compelling story if he is to extract any more money from Sal and his board of bean counters.

The situation is critical; his cash flow problem has become a biblical flood, and he needs an ark – fast. Desperation can be the mother of invention, and he recalls his conversation with Mae West about the struggles of the anonymous thousands of people in the movie business. It has given him the glimmer of an idea that might enable him to raise the money he needs. The scheme, cloaked under the guise of a charity, is so good he'd give himself a hug, if only his arms could extend around his vast girth. But first, he needs to talk to Elvis, hopefully when Priscilla is not there.

He walks into the auditorium as Elvis, the band, and the backing singers are running through the final number of the session. He's never been known to attend a rehearsal before – anything to do with his music and his performance is left entirely to Elvis – and the shock causes *Can't Help Falling in Love* to end abruptly in a discordant mess.

The band are confused and whisper amongst themselves, worried that he's a jinx, as in the old days if woman were to be seen on board a ship. They begin to shuffle towards the back of the stage, trying to put as much distance as possible between themselves and Colonel 'The Jonah' Parker.

He and Elvis sit in some seats towards the back of the auditorium where they won't be overheard.

"Elvis, I want to tell you something really important," he says.

"Whoa!" declares Elvis, holding up his hand as if he were trying to stop a horse. "Sir, will whatever you're going to say prevent me from going on holiday with Priscilla and Lisa Marie? Because, if it does, I don't want to hear another word."

"No," he replies, draping a fatherly arm across Elvis's shoulders. "It's just that I've become aware of something that has touched me deeply, and I was saying to Mrs Parker... er... or was it Bubba?... that I feel we must do something to help."

He explains that he and Elvis have had very successful careers in the movies, but there are so many others in the industry, such as actors, extras, technicians, and stagehands, who are experiencing hard times. He claims to have witnessed scenes that remind him of the Great Depression.

He blows his nose very loudly before adding, "Their plight has touched my heart, and yet without them, we can't make movies." He explains that he has one or two ideas about how they might extend a helping hand that he'd like to explore while Elvis is away on holiday. "I'm calling it my 'SOS Hollywood' project. Let's talk when you're back."

Elvis thinks, *He's up to something, but it's too soon to figure out what.*

Colonel Parker welcomes Elvis and Charlie Hodge, his old friend and faithful gofer, into his office at Graceland and waves them in the direction of a couple of chairs facing his desk.

"I hope you and the family had a great time in Hawaii and you've come back fully refreshed," he says. "And thanks for the postcard of Waikiki Beach and the message 'Wish You Were Here'." He puffs on his cigar, allowing the tension to build, before announcing that, as a result of a conversation he'd previously had with Elvis, he'd like to start a charity to help all those in Hollywood who've fallen on hard times.

"But, Colonel, sir, you always say you hate charities," Bubba, his assistant, protests. "You say they're a leech on honest businessmen such as yourself. I've never known you give so much as a dime to charity."

His response is to roar with laughter and assert that Bubba's memory must be failing him. "Oh dear, amnesia at such a young age."

"But I agree with Bubba, sir," interjects Elvis. "Just for the record, what was your last donation to a charity?"

"Hmm, I know my gift was something substantial." He closely

examines his cigar, to give himself time to think, before finally coming up with an answer. "Yes, I've got it. It was a home for retired carny folk."

Elvis, Bubba, and Charlie exchange unspoken glances of incredulity.

The Colonel outlines his plan to launch the SOS Hollywood charity with a show, to be staged in Las Vegas, called *Elvis Rocks the Movies*, which would see Elvis performing some of his biggest hits that have appeared in films, such as *Jailhouse Rock*, *Love Me Tender* and *Can't Help Falling in Love*.

"It sounds an excellent idea, but surely, sir, shouldn't it be held in Hollywood?" asks Elvis, who remains puzzled, although it's a worthy cause, why he's initiated such a project. Bubba is right; charities are an anathema to his manager. What's he up to?

"You see, son, the International Hotel has already given me, on behalf of the charity, a very large donation for the show to be held there. For the benefit of all those hard-pressed movie people we want to help, I felt compelled to accept their bid.

"And the NBC TV network has also made a substantial donation to the charity, via myself, to secure the rights to film the show and broadcast it at prime time over two nights."

Bubba points out that he's not aware of a Bank account having been opened in the name of the SOS Hollywood charity; for the record, where is the money being kept on deposit?

"In the safest possible place," he answers. "It's in my account with the Jefferson Davis Bank. Just for the time being. Naturally, I shall need to draw on some funds to cover certain expenses (the image of Mae West and her loan that he's repaying leaps to mind) before the funds are transferred to a new account."

Bubba raises a hand to ask a question. "Colonel Parker, sir, shouldn't trustees be appointed to run the affairs of the charity, particularly when so much money is involved?"

"Good point, Bubba. By the very nature of the word, trustee, we need people who are utterly trustworthy. Which is why I'm putting forward the names of myself, Elvis and his father, Vernon."

Elvis sighs and comments that he's already so busy that he doesn't know how he'll find the time to be a trustee.

"Don't worry, son. Folks will want to know that you're involved, but you can leave it all to the good ole Colonel to take care of business."

Understandably, he's very keen to move away from the topic of the financial arrangements as quickly as possible. He is telling them that he is lining up some big-name Hollywood stars to take part in the first half of the show when the phone on his desk starts to ring. He picks up the receiver and puts it down again to stop the call. The second half of the show, he continues, will feature Elvis singing songs from his movies.

The phone starts to ring again. The Colonel repeats the process of picking up and putting down the receiver, but almost immediately it starts ringing.

"Bubba, will you see who it is who keeps calling me and tell them that I'm in a conference and cannot be disturbed."

His young assistant stands by his desk and as he listens to the call, his mouth sags, and he looks horrified, as if he's seen a ghost.

He replaces the receiver.

"Colonel Parker, sir, Elvis, that was Mae West. She says she's grateful to you for repaying some of the loan, but she's concerned that she's heard nothing yet about when and where she'll be rehearsing with Elvis on the opening number of the show. She wants you to call back as soon as possible."

Elvis leaps to his feet, his chair falling back in the process. He is like a raging bull, and in his fury, he karate kicks the chair, reducing it to matchwood. "Me performing with Mae West! Are you mad? Not in a thousand years! Never! And what's this loan she's talking about?"

Colonel Parker opens his arms in a gesture of helplessness. "What could I do? The International and NBC both say, no, insist, they want her to open the show as one of the stars of the golden age of Hollywood. And if she's in the show, we'll get Cary Grant – yes, the Cary Grant – to be the host. My hands are tied. They're putting up a lot of money and we want to do the best we can for the charity."

"The King isn't happy," comments Charlie Hodge, with a shake of his head.

"Thank you, Charlie. I hadn't noticed," responds the Colonel, looking daggers at him.

"And what's all this about a loan?" demands Elvis.

He replies: "It was to cover a short-term cash flow problem while we were in Vegas." Elvis instinctively knows what it was for – to cover his gambling debts.

Bubba raises his hand. "There's one other thing I should tell you. Mae West mentioned that she's prepared a press release about her performing with Elvis in the show, and she wants you and Elvis to see it as a courtesy before she releases it."

Elvis lets out a Tarzan-like roar, one that will probably be heard by the animals in Memphis Zoo, and storms out of the office, slamming the door behind him.

The *Elvis Rocks the Movies* show is a huge success. Initially, Elvis felt angry and resentful at having to appear on stage with Mae West, a faded old film star, who is wearing too much make-up and an outrageously tight-fitting low-cut, gold dress that's entirely inappropriate for someone of her age; and that is one of life's great mysteries; for many years, she has always described herself as 'fortyish'.

Within 10 seconds it all changes. As soon as Jerry Lee Lewis starts playing the opening bars of *Great Balls of Fire*, the audience goes wild, and not just for Elvis and The Killer.

They take her to their hearts; she's a living legend and they love her chutzpah, for not being fazed or upstaged by performing with the two greatest ever rock and rollers.

With the audience stamping their feet, whistling, and demanding an encore, Elvis, Jerry Lee, and Mae go into a huddle and signal for Cary Grant, who is hosting the show, to sit at the piano alongside Jerry Lee as they launch into *Whole Lotta Shakin' Goin' On*.

Mae West begins to dance the hoochie coochie and Elvis, catching the mood, places his hands on her hips and they set off, dancing a conga across the stage. Cary Grant joins the line behind Elvis, and they conga into the audience, scores of whom fall in behind. A long line of dancers, trailing behind Mae West, wind their way through the auditorium before eventually returning to the stage.

It is a clip of the conga dance that makes the main news bulletins in America and then across the world. The show and the news coverage guarantee that Colonel Parker's SOS Hollywood charity is a million-dollar success.

Because Elvis is too busy to attend meetings of the trustees, he authorises Priscilla, much to Colonel Parker's disgust, to attend in his stead. Whenever applications for help and the distribution of funds are being considered, she is always accompanied by a hot-shot lawyer and an accountant.

The Colonel is disgruntled at the money being doled out to people he regards as slackers, when there are others, principally himself, who are more deserving. After all, it was his idea to set up the SOS

Hollywood charity and he should be entitled to some reward and to cover his expenses. But Priscilla and her two accomplices block all his requests.

Nevertheless, he cannot really complain, since he is the chief beneficiary of the charity. Although he'd lost track of how much he owed and to whom, all his debts have disappeared, submerged in the flood of donations to the charity.

RCA, Elvis's record label, thank their lucky stars that they agreed to record the show; the album which is subsequently released goes to the top of the charts.

And Mae West, having achieved icon status, follows up the success of the show with 'An Audience With...' tour. She is accompanied by Cary Grant who chats with her about her life in show business. The interview is interspersed with songs, including *Great Balls of Fire*, and performances of some of the best-loved scenes from her movies. Most popular of all, of course, are her anecdotes about her friendship with Elvis and the times they have worked together!

THE CHICKEN LIBERATION ARMY

"Colonel Parker, sir, I couldn't help noticing when I was walking into Graceland a moment ago that there's a six foot chicken marching up and down outside the Music Gates," Bubba, his assistant, tells him. "And this chicken is holding up a placard that says, 'The End is Nigh'."

The Colonel puffs meditatively on his cigar before making a token attempt to get up from the chair behind his desk; he is the third fattest man in the United States, so it is always going to be a struggle, and after five seconds he sinks back.

"Bubba, would you look out of the window to save me breaking my concentration while I study this invoice and tell me what the weather is like."

"Bright and sunny, sir."

"Just as I thought. The chicken seems to think the end is nigh, but I reckon Doomsday won't be today so we should get back to work. But we'll check the forecast for the next few days as a precaution. I'd hate to be caught out by hellfire and damnation," he chuckles, brushing away the layer of cigar ash that has accumulated down the front of his nuclear orange Hawaiian shirt.

"Hellfire and damnation – surely not you, Colonel. That's for the bad guys," says Bubba, managing to keep a straight face. "Shall I go down and try and find out what is going on?"

"No need. A man dressed up as a chicken and waving a placard – it must be a lunatic. If it becomes a problem, we'll send for the men in white coats."

But Colonel Parker and Bubba are not the only ones to have noticed what is happening at the Music Gates. Minnie Mae, peering out of the kitchen window while filleting a catfish, mentions the big chicken to Elvis, as he tucks into a slice of apple pie, an appetizer for lunch which is still two hours away.

"Is it Foghorn Leghorn?" he laughs.

"It could be but ah ain't sure."

Curious, Elvis gets up to take a look. His verdict is that he's the right colour – white – but a lot thinner and with a bigger head than Foghorn Leghorn.

"Ah'm a-gonna go an' git Grandpappy Hood's ole buffalo gun an' ah'll swear in court ah dun thought it wus a real chicken when ah go down there an' shoot at it."

"First things first," says Elvis, urging his grandmother to concentrate her efforts on lunch while they wait and see what happens.

When the big chicken returns the next day Bubba, on his own initiative, walks down to the Music Gates to find out what he is protesting about. He asks him why he is dressed up like that and what is the meaning of 'The End is Nigh' on his placard.

"I am the herald sent to warn you that your chickens are coming home to roost," he replies enigmatically before carrying on marching backwards and forwards outside the gates.

Nothing more happens until a letter addressed to Colonel Parker and Elvis arrives at Graceland. It is from the Chicken Liberation Army and demands that the Dixie Chickens who for years have had to endure the ignominy of performing as a chorus line of dancers, should be immediately released from their sentence of servitude to Colonel Parker.

Elvis, who is tainted by association with his manager, is therefore equally guilty of permitting such unchicken-like activities which must cease at once. The birds are to be released and provided with somewhere where they can live as normal chickens for the rest of their days.

Until this happens the activists demand the right to inspect the chickens' accommodation, both at Graceland and while on tour, their diet, medical facilities, and the stage on which they perform their dance routines. (*Goodness knows what will happen if they should discover that they dance on hot plate under a layer of straw*, thinks Colonel Parker to himself. *Things could turn ugly.*)

The letter concludes by urging that a meeting should be arranged immediately between Colonel Parker, Elvis, and a representative of the CLA to fully discuss these issues and how they can be resolved as quickly as possible. Unless such a meeting takes place within the next 48 hours, the CLA reserve the right to take whatever direct action is necessary in order to liberate the Dixie Chickens.

It ends: "You have been warned. The Cluck is Ticking."

"Are you comfortable wearing that costume?" asks Colonel Parker as someone dressed up as a chicken sits down in his office. "It can get very hot in here. I can ask my assistant, who is here to take notes, to open a window."

The representative of the Chicken Liberation Army who is attending the meeting with the Colonel and Elvis explains that the outfit is not only a disguise for security reasons, but it is also a badge of honour in their campaign to secure freedom for chickens.

"But I won't be nearly so hot and uncomfortable as your Dixie Chickens when they are performing," he goes on. "We hear stories that they are made to dance on a hot plate covered in straw. It sounds too cruel to be true, but such claims must be investigated."

Colonel Parker glances nervously at Elvis and starts to puff furiously on his cigar, like a locomotive building up a head of steam. He pulls out a handkerchief from the sleeve of his jacket to pat his reddening face and briefly removes his yellow straw trilby to fan himself.

Sensing his manager's anxiety to change the subject as quickly as possible, Elvis asks what they should call him.

"Officially, I suppose, I should be addressed as Chief Cockerel."

In his agitation the Colonel has been chewing the end of his cigar and is now concentrating on removing bits of tobacco from his mouth and his lips have turned a dark brown colour.

Elvis, who thought it would be a kindly gesture to wear his Aloha from Hawaii jumpsuit which features a large bald eagle on the front and back, the closest thing he could find in his wardrobe to a chicken, continues to take charge by asking what he would like to achieve from the meeting.

"For instance, do you have a pecking order?" he jokes, hoping to lighten the mood. It doesn't seem to work.

The Chief Cockerel replies that the first objective of their campaign is to obtain freedom for the Dixie Chickens. Given Elvis's links such a story will inevitably appear on TV news channels and front pages all around the world. When they win this victory, it will send a message that all chickens must be treated with dignity and respect.

"We want them to live naturally and happily and not have to perform like a chorus line of dancers or live in appalling battery houses. We are beginning our campaign right at the very top with the

Dixie Chickens and once we demonstrate that when Elvis and his manager acknowledge the rightness of our cause, we anticipate that many other exploiters of chickens will quickly follow suit."

By now Colonel Parker has recovered his composure and is in full bluster mode.

He tells him: "You sit there dressed up like a big chicken, making threats, but you know nothing."

He declares that the Dixie Chickens have a right to freedom of expression as guaranteed under the constitution of the United States of America, and that includes the right to perform as dancers.

Does he know, for example, that the tradition of dancing chickens dates back to the time of the Pilgrim Fathers? No, of course he doesn't! In those early days at Plymouth Rock, times were as hard as their Puritan principles, and the only entertainment that was permitted was to train some chickens that had come with them on the Mayflower to dance. It was seen by the Pilgrim Fathers as harmless fun.

He declares: "It is a tradition which could have been lost in the mists of time but which I have been proud to preserve – never mind the cost that I have had to bear. An important part of our heritage has been safe in my hands for which, I believe, Americans will be profoundly grateful and will want to continue to be entertained by the Dixie Chickens. They will not allow you or your organisation to tear out the pages of dancing chickens from the history books of the United States of America."

The Chief Cockerel, stands up, makes a few clucking noises, flaps his wings, and heads for the door of the office in a slow, stiff-legged chicken fashion. He pauses to say, "You will hear from us again." His exit from the office was pure Norman Collier; the famed chicken impersonator could not have bettered it.

"Oh wow!" exclaims Elvis. "I didn't know all that stuff about the Pilgrim Fathers and the history of dancing chickens. It was really interesting."

The Colonel nods his head, smiles and puffs on his cigar. "It's the first rule of carny. It might be hogwash but tell it like it's true."

In the 1950s, Elvis's concerts were characterised by fans who screamed, fainted, danced in the aisles, and rushed the stage to try and touch him. Sometimes he was mobbed and had his clothes ripped off. In the 1970s, when he returned to performing live, the behaviour of his fans was more restrained; there was no stampede to the front of the stage. Fans formed a polite procession, saying to each other "No, after you," or "Please, you go first."

Which makes one particular concert of all the 1,684 that Elvis performed in his lifetime, unique. It was the only one where he and the band had to stop the show and leave the stage because of a riot between his fans and a flock of people dressed as chickens.

The concert begins in the usual way with the TCB band playing *2001: A Space Odyssey* followed by Elvis running on stage to sing *C C Rider* immediately followed by *I Got A Woman*. Again, as usual, he pauses to walk to the front centre of the stage for a chat with the audience.

He sees a group of about 100 people all dressed as chickens sitting together in the front centre aisle. It is such an extraordinary sight that he is nonplussed and tries to make a couple of admittedly rather feeble jokes.

Then one of the chickens stands up and crows 'cock-a-doodle-doo'. It is a signal for all the others to get up and start to leave their seats. As they make their way to the area in front of the stage, they start to nod their heads as if looking for corn seed, scratching at the ground with their feet and making loud clucking noises.

Elvis appeals to them go back to their seats, but they ignore him and unfurl a 100 ft long banner that declares in bright red letters: 'Free the Dixie Chickens'. It is a slogan that means absolutely nothing to 99 per cent of the audience who are becoming increasingly angry and abusive. Some of them have travelled hundreds of miles to be able to say they've fulfilled the wish of a lifetime to see Elvis perform live, while everyone without exception has paid top dollar to watch the show.

When one of the chickens climbs some steps at the side of the stage, pecking as he goes, as if following a trail of corn, Kathy Westmoreland and the Sweet Inspirations begin to scream in fear of their lives. Immediately Elvis runs over to stand in front of them and go into his karate kill stance; Charlie Hodge, his oldest friend and chief gofer, hurries to position himself in front of Elvis, prepared to take a peck, if need be, to save him.

The fury of the Elvis fans erupts; some of them rush forward to drag the chicken off the stage while others wade into the rest of the flock of chickens to try and tear down the banner.

Elvis and the band are ushered away as feathers fly in what becomes a full-scale riot. It is half an hour before the police and stewards can remove all the chickens from the auditorium and the concert can resume with Elvis changing the set list to perform *A Riot in Cell Block Number 9* and *Jailhouse Rock* to cheers from the audience. The local police chief announces later: "The chickens will roost for the night in the police cells and be charged later."

Colonel Parker is desperately worried as he sits in his office at Graceland and reads the latest communication from the Chicken Liberation Army. The letter states: 'We may have lost a battle, but the war goes on'. If they can cause a riot at an Elvis concert, what else might they be prepared to do, he reasons.

The events at the concert give a huge boost to the Chicken Liberation Army's campaign to improve the welfare of chickens. Images of battery farms and film clips of the Dixie Chickens dancing feature in the media, together with interviews with the CLA's Chief Cockerel who continues to appear in his chicken outfit.

The campaign strikes a chord with Mr and Mrs America, and almost overnight sales of chicken meat and eggs plummet at supermarkets like Safeway, Walmart and Piggly Wiggly. Particularly hard hit by the backlash are the Kentucky Fried Chicken restaurants, to such an extent that Colonel Sanders himself rings Colonel Parker to plead with him to help resolve the situation by announcing the immediate retirement of the Dixie Chickens who initially provoked the campaign and, as far as he is concerned, remain its chief focus.

"Thank you for the call, Harland," Colonel Parker tells him. "The Dixie Chickens are beloved by their thousands of fans. They are part of that great tradition of showbiz, up there with George M Cohan, Al Jolson, Jack Benny and Elvis. What if I were to suggest that you stop serving chicken in your restaurants? I'm sure that would do a lot to appease these terrorists."

"That's impossible, Tom, but I don't know what we can do to stop them. I want to save my business as much as you do your act."

"We cannot give in to their demands," he responds. "Who knows where it will end or what other idiots they will inspire to start protesting about some other great American institution. I'll say this, Harland: sooner or later these clowns will put a foot wrong and that will be our chance."

In the meantime, he has an idea. They hide their identities by dressing up as chickens. But where do they get all these costumes from? If they can find out who the supplier is, they might learn their names. He'll contact his carny friends and asks Colonel Sanders to get his marketing people to make inquiries.

"Let's reveal their true identities, put their lives under the microscope and see how they like it," adds Colonel Parker. "We'll talk again soon."

While he still refuses to announce that the Dixie Chickens will stop performing, he is conscious of the threat made by the Chicken Liberation Army that they reserve the right to take direct action to achieve their goal. Who knows what that means, but it could be very unpleasant, so he calls a meeting to devise a plan of action to protect them.

Priscilla insists: "I refuse to have them in the house and, anyway, they're the Colonel's responsibility and not mine!" She sets her mouth, folds her arms and glares at everybody else in the room as if to say that's settled. Nobody challenges the Tiny Terror.

"If that is the case, then we need to mount a twenty-four-hour guard on the coop where the Dixie Chickens are being kept in the grounds at Graceland," says the Colonel.

"I want to volunteer," declares Elvis. "I'm not afraid of big chickens." He makes his point by executing a couple of karate chops and adds, "No, sir!"

His manager thanks him for the offer but says that sadly he must say no. "They might look like something out of a Warner Brothers cartoon, but they are terrorists, desperate people. Who knows what they might do. We cannot afford anything to happen to you, Elvis. Think of the panic in Las Vegas and Hollywood. And not to mention Wall Street. It could cause a run on the banks."

"And they might decide to kidnap Elvis instead of the Dixie Chickens," says Charlie Hodge helpfully.

The idea of Elvis standing guard is rejected, and so is the offer of Minnie Mae, on account of her age and her tendency to shoot first and ask questions later. They might be terrorists, but nobody wants there to be a massacre.

"Surely, Colonel Parker, the answer is obvious," interjects Elvis. "Who is in charge of security at Graceland? It's Red and Sonny."

Knowing what might happen the West cousins have remained silent and invisible during the discussion, making sure they are well hidden behind Lamar Fike, which is quite easy to do, given his vast fatness.

"Are Red and Sonny here?" wonders Elvis, standing up to look around the room. "Yes, there they are. Okay, boys, we're putting you in charge."

The West boys never like to move far from the Jungle Room where

they can sit all day and sip beer, read the funny papers, and take a nap when it all gets too much for them.

Once, when Charlie Hodge had had enough, he complained bitterly about all the housework he had to do at Graceland while they lounged about all day.

They tell him: "We're at Elvis's beck and call and on duty around the clock. We must be like coiled springs, ready to leap into action at a moment's notice." With that they pop another can of beer.

However, they have spent the last couple of nights standing guard outside the chicken coop, shivering in the cold. They stamp their feet and blow on their hands while imagining Elvis and the other guys sitting warm and cosy in the Jungle Room, eating pizza, drinking beer, and watching TV.

Reluctantly, Colonel Parker gives in to their moans; the chickens must be protected, but who else will do it? His best option is to agree to let them have a fire, a couple of armchairs, blankets, beer, and a radio that they tune to a country music station.

So far it has been another quiet, relaxing night until Red, reaching for a beer from the cooler box, looks up and sees – looming into the light given off by the fire – a giant chicken, wearing a Lone Ranger-style mask and carrying an empty sack. He leaps to his feet and shouts in alarm, rousing his cousin Sonny, asleep in his armchair.

When another half a dozen masked chickens approach, the West cousins yell: "Run! We're outnumbered! Let's get help!"

They pause on their way back to the house to confer. Nobody can blame them; they did the right thing; they didn't stand a chance as there must have been at least a dozen of them. Yes, they are in agreement; that's sorted out the facts.

They wake up everybody who's asleep in Graceland – apart from Elvis who, given the odd hours he keeps, hasn't gone to bed yet – with the shocking news that the Chicken Liberation Army is attempting to kidnap the Dixie Chickens.

"So, what are you doing here?" shouts the Colonel, who has appeared in his International Hotel towel dressing gown. "You're supposed to be in charge of security and guarding them."

"We tried to fight them off," protest the West boys. "But we were overwhelmed. There must have been at least twenty of those masked chickens. We fought a rearguard action, but it was a losing battle. What else could we do?"

"Your job!" snarls an exasperated Colonel Parker, who is clearly doubtful of how much of a struggle they put up. "And what do you expect us to do – head them off at the pass." He shakes his head. "I should have put Old Shep (Elvis's dog) in charge. At least he might have kept them at bay with his fleas."

A group of them, including Minnie Mae who is armed with Grandpappy Hood's old buffalo gun, return to the coop to confirm their worst fears that the Dixie Chickens have been kidnapped. Much to their disgust, the West cousins discover that their remaining supplies of beer cans were also taken.

A couple of days later a letter addressed to Colonel Parker and Elvis arrives from the Chicken Liberation Army, informing them that the Dixie Chickens have been released on a free-range farm near Memphis that is home to at least 100,000 white chickens. There they are hidden in plain sight and impossible for the Colonel to find amongst so many identical birds. 'We have given them their freedom and the opportunity to live the rest of their lives like happy, normal chickens,' states the letter. 'We are sure that all our supporters who share the beliefs of the Chicken Liberation Army will applaud this action. We will announce the next target of our campaign soon. Organisations that don't treat chickens with respect should be very afraid.'

Elvis calls at the Colonel's office later to offer his condolences about the fate of the Dixie Chickens. Rather than enjoying their freedom, he wonders how they will survive the hurly burly of farm life, competing for food and somewhere to roost at night with all those other rough and ready chickens when they have lived such a cosseted life with the Colonel?

Elvis expects to find him devastated, since it was a dancing chickens act that got him started in carny many years ago, and since then, for largely sentimental reasons, Elvis suspects, he has always continued with some new incarnation of that original act. Over the ensuing years he has managed singers like Gene Austin, Eddy Arnold, Hank Snow and Elvis himself, all major stars. But he has never forgotten his roots and how he got started in show business, always maintaining a dancing chickens act, one which has been known in recent years as the Dixie Chickens.

He doesn't look heartbroken. In fact, he's as busy as a worker bee. He is on the phone to Colonel Sanders, hurriedly scribbling notes on the back of an invoice. "Hold on a minute, Harland," he says as Bubba rushes in to say that Schwab's store in Memphis have said that of course, as it's for Elvis, they can borrow a truck. It will be outside the front door in 30 minutes.

Then he is on the phone to Lamar Fike. "Will it be ready in the next half an hour? Excellent! Bring it round and fix it to the truck and then we'll be ready to go."

The Colonel pats his face with a grubby-looking handkerchief and says to Elvis: "Will you drive the truck?" He smiles and adds, "I know it's been a while since you drove one, but I'd be grateful."

He explains that thanks to Bubba, they have learned by a process of elimination that the Dixie Chickens were released on a farm 10 miles outside Memphis. However, they need to move quickly because it is not the sort of place where chickens live for very long before becoming being processed into joints and wrapped in cellophane. The farmer has agreed to suspend operations for half a day while they carry out their search.

"But Colonel, sir, it will be impossible to find them," Elvis tells him. "Five chickens amongst a hundred thousand other birds that all look the same. That's tougher than searching for a needle in a haystack – a hopeless cause. Please don't build your hopes up, expecting a miracle. You must prepare yourself for the worst."

"Just wait and see," he chuckles, leaving Elvis feeling mystified.

Elvis drives the truck onto the farm and sees ahead of him fields covered in a white, moving carpet of clucking, head-bobbing chickens.

"Where do we start?"

"Okay, Lamar, hit the button," declares Colonel Parker. "Now watch very carefully."

Lamar has rigged up an amplifier to a tape recorder that plays *Sweet Georgia Brown* – the signature tune of the Dixie Chickens – on a loop. It is the tune with which they begin every performance, like Elvis does with *C C Rider*.

"Look, over there!" yells Bubba excitedly. Some 75 yards away, on hearing the music, a chicken has gone into a high-stepping dance routine. "It's one of the Dixie Chickens!" He takes a sack to collect her and bring her back to the truck. Within three-quarters of an hour they have rounded up the other four chickens in the troupe and are heading back to Graceland.

Colonel Parker tells Elvis that Colonel Sanders' people have been able to discover the identity of the leader of the Chicken Liberation Army from the company that supplied him with all the chicken costumes. The next step will be to organise a press conference which he'd like Elvis to attend.

It is held in a suite at the Peabody Hotel and the room is packed with journalists, TV crews and cameramen.

Colonel Parker begins by addressing them as 'My Fellow Americans' and Elvis is unable to stop himself from flinching and blushing on hearing such a statement from his manager, considering the very credible rumours that he is an illegal alien.

Given the importance of the press conference the Colonel has dressed more formally than usual; it's his regular baggy grey suit but instead of a Hawaiian shirt he is wearing a red checked shirt and a dark tie patterned with small roulette wheels. He thought about having a shave, but the number and size of his jowls meant it would have taken up the best part of a day. Besides, it makes him look careworn from having devoted so many hours striving to rescue his beloved Dixie Chickens.

"First let me give you the good news that all their fans are waiting to hear: the Dixie Chickens are safe and well, and the art of chicken dancing will live on."

Some of the journalists, having been suitably 'rewarded' in advance by the Colonel, begin to loudly applaud, and this encourages the others to join in. It makes for good TV, as well he knew it would.

He affects to be visibly moved by the applause, dabbing at the corner of an eye, while eventually raising a hand and asking them to stop.

The Colonel decides to play down the outrage and go for a more sorrowful indignation as he reminds them that the terrorists belonging to the Chicken Liberation Army claim that they care about the freedom and welfare of chickens.

"No, they don't!" he roars, banging his fist on the desk. "They dumped the Dixie Chickens on a farm that supplies the Cheap Cheep-Cheep Chicken Company with joints of chicken breasts and drumsticks wrapped in cellophane for sale in corner stores. That's how much they care about their welfare!"

There is a loud gasp from the journalists.

He then holds up a photograph of a man's face; it looks like a police mugshot with a row of numbers at the bottom. Bubba hands out copies to all the journalists.

"This is the face of a terrorist – Al Capon, the leader of the Chicken Liberation Army, the man who calls himself the Chief Cockerel," says Colonel Parker, who condemns him as a draft dodger, convicted thief and a man who has abandoned his wife and three young children.

"Oh, and I nearly forgot. He is also fraudster, having failed to pay for the chicken outfits he obtained for his thugs."

Colonel Parker points to Elvis sitting beside him at the table. "When the call came did Elvis dodge the draft? No, sir. He stood up like a true American patriot and went to serve with the Army in Germany to hold the line against the communists. He was the King of Rock and Roll, but he served his time without complaint."

He once more shows the picture of Al Capon. "What did this man do when he was drafted? He hid himself in a chicken outfit. Then he and his gang tried to wreck one of Elvis's shows, he kidnapped America's last surviving dancing chickens act, and he tried to hoodwink the American people into refusing to buy chicken products and sabotaging the businesses of such great organisations as Walmart, Safeway, Piggly Wiggly and Kentucky Fried Chicken. I say we are well rid of Mr Al Capon and his Chicken Liberation Army!"

He concludes the press conference by saying that he has handed over all the information he has on the CLA and its leader to the police.

As the journalists begin to leave the room one reporter stands up and asks him about the allegations of foul play that have been circulating in the wake of the Chicken Liberation Army's campaign, in particular, that the Dixie Chickens actually dance on a hot plate covered in straw. Can Colonel Parker confirm or deny this?

The exodus pauses, and the reporters all turn to face him to await his answer. Cameras are switched back on and notebooks are opened.

"Ho ho ho," laughs the Colonel, slipping into Father Christmas mode. "Wait till I tell that one to Jack Benny. He's sure to use it in his next show." Nothing more is said, and he is still laughing as he and Elvis walk out of the door behind them.

Al Capon decides to follow a policy of hiding in plain sight and opts for somewhere nobody will think of looking for him. But such is the hue and cry that has been whipped up by Colonel Parker that a sharp-eyed member of the public spots him frying chicken in a KFC restaurant in St Louis.

After his arrest he 'sings like a canary' and divulges the names of his accomplices who were involved in the riot at Elvis's show and the kidnapping of the Dixie Chickens.

Elvis smiles as he asks his manager what plans he has for the troupe to cash in on all the publicity that has been generated. Should they hot foot it on tour, perhaps, or go for a TV special?

Colonel Parker gives him an old-fashioned look. "That's a very good suggestion, Elvis," he replies. "But with all this silly nonsense about hot plates – what will people think of next? – it may be best if they enjoy some rest and recuperation first."

THE WORLD'S RAREST ANIMAL

It's quiz time at Graceland and Minnie Mae has asked them if they know what meat is in the stew they are eating. There is always an element of risk involved in Elvis's grandmother's down-home style of cooking, and they all look nervously at each other around the dining table, wondering what it could be. They would have much preferred to be asked the question before they started.

Having dined on the likes of raccoon, muskrat, squirrel, and alligator they consider themselves to be battle-hardened. What on earth could it be this time?

Aunt Delta takes a swig from her cocktail shaker – she has dispensed with using a glass as being superfluous – and declares: "Ah knows wut it ain't – an' it sure ain't raccoon cuz that can be tough an' chewy. This meat's jest too good ter be raccoon."

Minnie Mae confirms that her daughter is right, and it isn't raccoon. "C'mon an' see if'n any of yer can guess wut it is. All ah'm a-sayin' is yer gonna be mighty surprised!"

"It tastes like prime Texas beef," says Elvis, who seems to be enjoying it, so all the other guys, hearing with relief that it could be beef, follow his lead with nods of the head and murmurs of appreciation.

Dr Nick, Elvis's personal physician, thinks it tastes delicious and says it reminds him of a Greek goulash.

"More like a Greek ghoul," mutters Colonel Parker under his breath.

"Eat up everybody. Goulash is good for the bowels," recommends Dr Nick who, through his work in looking after Elvis and his problems with constipation, regards himself as a world leading authority on such matters.

"Well, I must say, Dodger (the name Elvis sometimes calls his grandmother) I'm not sure what it is but it certainly does taste good," and he hands over his plate for an extra helping. Minnie Mae folds her arms and beams as she looks around the table, feeling pleased with herself, before revealing that it's goat's meat, which she has served in a stew with maple syrup dumplings, sweet potatoes, and turnip tops. "Who'd like some more?"

There is a muffled chorus of coughing and shuffling on chairs as everybody but Elvis, who asks if he can have the last two dumplings as well, tries to indicate that they are full and couldn't possibly eat another thing.

He supposes that goat meat is not something you can normally buy at the Piggly Wiggly supermarket downtown and inquires where his grandmother was able to get it.

Minnie Mae tells them that she saw a goat roaming around Graceland. Although she was puzzled as to how it could have got into the grounds, she didn't intend to miss out on such a piece of good fortune. She shot it while it was grazing under the trees where the turkeys are usually to be found. Afterwards she skinned and butchered it herself.

"Are you sure, Minnie Mae, that it was a goat?" questions Priscilla who, as usual, has opted to give the stew a miss in favour of a carefully assembled mixed leaf salad of well under 100 calories.

"Well, it had horns an' four legs jest like a goat," she replies.

Priscilla hopes she is right and has not forgotten that Graceland, with its 19 acres of land and secure fencing, is currently looking after a number of wild animals while improvements are being made at Memphis Zoo. One of the animals for which they are providing a temporary home is a Swahili antelope, of which there are only 10 surviving in the whole world. It is the zoo's most prized possession and the subject of a special campaign by the famous British TV presenter and naturalist David Carruthers. In fact, the antelope is known as Dave after him and will respond to its name when called.

"I don't suppose you happened to call out 'Dave' before you shot him?" asks Priscilla, shaking her head sorrowfully.

"No, we didn't say howdy," says Minnie Mae, who admits that it slipped her mind about the zoo animals they were looking after. She saw what she thought was a goat and reached for her gun without thinking.

There is a stunned silence in the room, as they try to take on board the consequences of what they have just heard, that they – including Elvis – have just eaten the world's rarest animal. Pandas are ten-a-penny compared to Swahili antelopes like Dave. How do they explain away its demise? And what if Dave was the last surviving male? Does that mean the species is now irrevocably doomed?

Colonel Parker is already suffering from a severe dose of indigestion, brought on by knowing what he has just eaten and the worry of trying to find a way to mitigate this disaster.

Life has been a vale of tears for the Swahili antelopes that once roamed the Masai Mara game reserve in their tens of thousands. Within a generation its habitat, particularly the bushes, whose leaves formed the principal part of its diet, disappeared to make way for the ever-increasing number of coffee plantations being developed by Barista Coffee U-like Inc.

And if that was not bad enough, it was hunted for its meat which is likened to fillet steak and is therefore much in demand by both the tribesmen and Michelin starred restaurants. Its horns are ground to produce what the Swahili people – and the Chinese – believe to be a powerful aphrodisiac; and its hide makes hard-wearing rugs such as the one in the Jungle Room, as Elvis was embarrassed to learn later.

Once a Swahili antelope has been killed there is not much left after the tribesmen have finished with it, apart from the hooves; and even then, these are often made into ashtrays for the tourists.

Dave was no more than a few weeks old and more dead than alive when he was found in the bush by David Carruthers during the making of a television documentary; realising his importance as one of the last survivors of this near extinct species, he hand-reared him and saved his life. As a result, a strong father-son bond was forged between them.

The famous naturalist would spend hours communing with Dave, lying on the ground near him, saying the occasional soothing words, and offering him apples and grapes. Once the antelope was near fully grown, he set about carefully finding a home, eventually selecting Memphis Zoo based on criteria such as the standard of care and the size of the paddock, but most of all, the guarantee of preferential super star status that would be given to Dave and his welfare.

Elvis is distraught at what has happened and dreads the kind of headlines that could appear should the news leak out, with most of them linking his name with words like 'killer', 'innocent victim', 'eaten for dinner', 'heartbroken naturalist', and 'world's rarest animal', all printed in big black capital letters.

What makes it so awful is that no one cares more about animals than Elvis who has his own much-loved menagerie that includes his stable of horses, a pet chimpanzee, an old fleabag of a dog and a flock of turkeys. Even Colonel Parker's retired dancing chickens, having been replaced by a new troupe, have found a home there instead of being handed over to Kentucky Fried Chicken, as was Colonel Parker's plan.

Elvis was very happy for Memphis Zoo to use the grounds of Graceland as a temporary home for some of their animals free of charge. "They'll be safe here," he remembers himself saying.

"What can be done to put things right, Colonel?" he laments, wringing his hands. "What happened to that poor creature is a crime and I'm going to have to stand up, take responsibility and admit it at my trial."

The prospect of any sort of trial or inquiry causes the Colonel to groan deeply as he sits in his office behind his old-fashioned dark wood desk, puffing furiously at his cigar and mopping his brow with a dingy-looking handkerchief. He morosely pulls the lever of the gaming machine that he keeps there to see if a win will inspire him, but up pop three bars with the word 'Loser' on each one. "That's the way things are running at the moment," he sighs.

His assistant Bubba urges him not to despair. Maybe they can mount an expedition to capture one of the remaining nine Swahili antelopes still in the wild and smuggle it back to Graceland before anyone finds out the truth.

The Colonel laughs bitterly. "Can you imagine, if we send someone like Charlie Hodge, the great white hunter, to be let loose in Africa? I mean to say, just think about it for a moment. He'd either get lost and have to be rescued like Dr Livingstone, or he'd come back with a hyena with a limp that the tribesmen conned him into buying."

Elvis, who is consoling himself by snacking on a box of iced donuts, looks up and says, "I've been thinking. Minnie Mae shot the antelope because it looked like a goat. Maybe, just maybe, we can find a goat from somewhere that looks like Dave the antelope."

"It's just an idea," he adds, and his gaze returns to the box and selecting his next donut.

But for Colonel Parker it is as if someone has lit the fuse of a firework. "That's it!" he explodes. "Of course, you're so right Elvis. That's what we need – a lookalike goat, like a stunt double in the movies."

He remembers one of his old carny colleagues who runs an act called 'Billy the Kid – the Wild West's Wildest Goat'. "Jimmy Toggenburg will have plenty of goats and one of them could be a match," he says. He tells Bubba to find a photograph of Dave from the Memphis Zoo guide and to send it to Jimmy together with a couple of hundred dollars.

"As much as that, sir?"

The Colonel shrugs his shoulders. "We're in a tough spot. We need to buy ourselves some time while we try to figure out a solution." After a moment's reflection, he says, "But you're right. Make it a hundred and fifty dollars."

"Even afterwards, won't it still look more like a goat than an antelope?" wonders Bubba.

"Leave it to Jimmy. He'll fix it."

Time is of the essence, they learn the next day, because David Carruthers is planning to visit Graceland with a crew to film the Swahili antelope in its new temporary home. Apart from St Francis of Assisi, nobody has done more to promote the care of animals than the famous naturalist.

Dave, the Swahili antelope, will be the star of a new documentary, designed to tug at heart strings and cheque books, about the importance of protecting extremely rare animals in the wild so that they are not lost to the world forever.

"Ah'm powerful sorry ah dun shot that antelope," Minnie Mae confesses to her daughter, Aunt Delta. "But ah could-a sworn it wus a goat. Ah had no trouble a-pickin' out them zebras we got a-roamin' around Graceland, an' them ugly looking things they walk around with."

"They'se called gnus, Ma. An' that's the good gnus – you didn't shoot one o' them," she cackles.

"Elvis is real upset," continues Minnie Mae. "But it do seem a cryin' shame ter waste all that meat that ah've got a-goin' spare in the freezer, an' a-seein' how we wus allus raised ter waste nuthin'."

She plans to make a meat loaf with lots of seasoning and onion gravy, as well as some sausages. "Folks ain't gonna know it's the antelope an' ah surely ain't gonna tell 'em," she declares.

The imposter antelope is ready just in time for the announcement that David Carruthers and his film crew are on their way. A similar sized goat with the right kind of grey-brown colouring is delivered by the Colonel's old carny pal; Charlie Hodge, Elvis's chief booster and gofer, is put to work with a pair of scissors and some very strong glue to remove the goat's beard and to stick on the horns that formerly adorned the head of Dave. But it is still a long way from being a convincing stunt double that they were hoping for.

"It looks a bit on the small side to me," considers Elvis, who has grave doubts that it will fool an expert like David Carruthers. "Do we have a Plan B, Colonel Parker?" he inquires.

"I'm working on it, but for as long as possible, and hopefully until this naturalist guy gives up and leaves, I think it's got to involve not letting him get too close and only seeing it when it's dark outside."

Meanwhile, he has been in touch with his network of carny and circus contacts to see if there is any way of getting one of the remaining Swahili antelopes still in the wild to be brought to Graceland as quickly as possible as a substitute for Dave. He has difficulty forming the words but finally blurts out: "Whatever it costs!"

There's a gasp because these are words they have never heard Colonel Parker utter before. He adds: "Please make it fast and be discreet."

As soon as he arrives at Graceland the world-famous naturalist is impatient to meet up with his old friend the Swahili antelope and see how he is enjoying his temporary surroundings.

"I'm so looking forward to seeing him again," he says. "It seems ages since we last saw each other. What a reunion it will be."

The Colonel frowns and adopts the pose of Rodin's Thinker except, of course, the statue isn't of a man who is the size of a walrus, who smokes a cigar and wears a straw trilby. After much pondering he slowly shakes his head in what he hopes is a philosophical way.

"It might be hard to find him, Mr Carruthers," he says. "Maybe it is all the extra space here at Graceland that he can roam around in. And, of course, it is all a bit new and strange to him. I think he has become very shy and taken to hiding himself in distant corners of the grounds."

He nods towards Elvis who notes his cue and adds, "It might be best to try and see him when it starts to get dark. That's when we might get to see him when he's feeling less nervous."

"I must say, Mr Presley, that it is very kind of you to let me and my film crew come to Graceland to see our special VIP Swahili antelope," says David Carruthers. "It is so good of you to look after him like this, as well as some other animals from the zoo. Very public spirited indeed. I shall write about it in our next newsletter.

"In the meantime, we'll follow your advice and wait until the

light starts to fade before going out to find him. Over the years we've made several programmes about him, and he and I have become very close friends. He recognises me and will come and feed from my hand. I know you're concerned that he's become a bit shy here, being away from his usual surroundings at the zoo, but I'm sure he will respond at once when I call his name. Just you wait and see; he'll come rushing up to say hello. Afterwards he'll be fine to do his stuff for the cameras."

He laughs: "One-take Dave, we call him."

Minnie Mae has been advised that it would be hospitable to prepare a typical English meal for their famous guest. To make conversation while waiting for it to be served, Elvis wonders if he would also like to meet Scatter, his pet chimpanzee, and Old Shep, his dog. He thinks about it for a long time, smiles wanly, and then says, "Of course, but perhaps that is a treat I can save for another day. I need to focus all my thoughts on Dave."

He feels this new documentary, especially given the role of Elvis and Graceland, will generate massive publicity in helping the campaign to protect the world's rarest animal. His whole face lights up and he smiles broadly. "Wow! I've had this wonderful idea. We should film a close-up sequence of Elvis and me with Dave. Imagine the interest that will generate in our project. And we can use a still for posters of the documentary and for the cover of special calendars."

"Huh huh," says Elvis, fiddling with the fringes of his jumpsuit and looking nervously across at Colonel Parker.

He is spared from having to come up with a more meaningful conversation by the entrance of Minnie Mae with her version of a typical English dinner – sausages, sweet potato fries, and black-eyed peas. There is also meat loaf with onion gravy as an alternative, she announces.

"From what we hear, Mr Carruthers, folks in England eat sausages and fries nearly every day," comments Charlie.

"This meal does look appetising, but I must tell you that I'm a vegetarian," he says. "I love animals and I have too much respect for them to want to eat them. May I follow Priscilla's example and have a salad."

Minnie Mae is nonplussed and about to say something, but she sees a warning shake of the head from Priscilla.

The TV crew report that they have made an initial search of the grounds of Graceland but there were no sightings of the Swahili antelope. This is not a surprise because he is being kept locked up in a loft above the stables with Vernon, Elvis's father, for company; he is under orders only to escort him into the grounds when it starts to get dark and stick to the out-of-the-way places.

David Carruthers, dressed in his signature safari suit and desert boots, and the film crew are ready to set off in search of Dave, accompanied by Elvis and Charlie. Wishing to add a note of caution to the proceedings, Colonel Parker tells them: "Don't be too disappointed if you don't find him at first. Everybody at Graceland will assure you that he's very happy here and he's probably just playing hide and seek and having a bit of fun in an antelope sort of way."

"Maybe he wants an early night, and we should let him rest in peace," suggests Elvis, who then realises his blunder using the phrase 'rest in peace' and hopes nobody notices.

After an hour of searching, all they have accomplished is to wake up the turkeys and Colonel Parker's former troupe of dancing chickens and cause a stampede of zebras and gnus that flattens the rose garden.

Elvis suggests they should call it a day and return to the house for supper, but David Carruthers is determined to keep on looking. Every half minute or so he calls out "Dave" and walks with an apple in his outstretched hand. Suddenly he motions for everyone to stop.

"Shush, I think that's him over there," he whispers, holding a finger to his lips.

He turns to the film crew and tells them to stay very quiet but to keep the camera rolling. The Swahili antelope might be nervous until he recognises him. He moves forward cautiously, calling out "Dave, Dave" and holding out the apple.

The cameraman, who is looking through a powerful lens, warns him that the antelope is pawing the ground and has a funny look in his eye. The signs are that he is getting angry.

"No, everything is fine," he reassures them. "He's just showing how pleased he is to see me."

Moments later it lowers its head and charges. The naturalist turns to run but has hardly gone a few paces before he is butted from behind and sent flying by the antelope that keeps on running in the direction of the Music Gates.

Later, once the Swahili antelope is rounded up, Vernon is told he must be kept in the loft above the stables until further notice. "And what about me?" he asks.

"You, too," insists the Colonel.

"I simply don't understand it," complains David Carruthers, as he sits perched on two red satin 'I Love Elvis' cushions on a chair in the kitchen while Priscilla tends to a few scrapes and bruises.

"I've known him for years and this is so out of character. He's never done anything like this before."

"Perhaps it's because of the new surroundings," suggests Priscilla helpfully as she dabs on a little iodine. He's been urged to put himself under the care of Dr Nick, Elvis's personal physician for a few days, in the hope this would buy more time, but he declines, saying he won't rest until he's reunited with Dave.

He'll be lucky, thinks Colonel Parker.

"I do hope he's all right," continues the famous naturalist. "If I know Dave, he is probably feeling very sorry for himself after what happened."

"Maybe it was the wrong kind of apple, and he didn't like the look of it," says Elvis. "Let's try a golden delicious when we go out again."

THE PRESLEY TURNIP PATCH

Bubba, Colonel Parker's assistant, picks up the phone, looks puzzled and calls out: "Sir, there's a Mr Presley on the phone."

"If it's Elvis, put him through."

"There's a problem, sir, because I don't think it is. He doesn't sound anything like Elvis," Bubba, informs him. "And I'm pretty sure it's not Vernon."

"Then get rid of him. Tell him he's got the wrong number. You can see how busy I am," he says as he drops another token into the gaming machine he keeps beside his desk.

"He claims he's related to Elvis, sir."

"Oh no, not another one. It's always the same. They say their name is Presley, they're down on their luck and they need a handout. Dammit, now see what's happened." He looks on in despair as two gold discs are followed by a turkey in the window of the gaming machine; he was so close, but he loses again. As he invariably does.

"He says his name is Eli Presley, sir."

The Colonel sighs and shakes his head and tells his assistant to say they'll call him back.

"But he's in a pay phone booth, sir."

"Bubba, take the number and then put the phone down right away. Whatever that number is, once you've written it down, put it in the wastepaper bin. I mean, we're trying to run a multi-million-dollar business here not a welfare office."

Later, a little voice in his head whispers, *'What if he is related to Elvis and he really does need help?'* As a precaution he decides to check with Minnie Mae, Elvis's grandmother, to see if she has ever heard of an Eli Presley. She's the one member of the family who is most likely to know.

He has another go on the gaming machine and, to his disgust, up pop three turkeys, and he loses again. All the signs are that it is going to be a bad day.

It is early evening when he walks into the kitchen where Minnie Mae is making Elvis's breakfast. He has not been up long and to pass the time he nibbles on a flapjack while Dodger, a name he sometimes calls his grandmother, prepares a stack of pancakes that will be served with blueberry sauce, fresh cream, and honey.

Colonel Parker asks her if she's heard of an Eli Presley who claims to be related to Elvis. She shakes her head and says the name doesn't mean anything to her and she cannot recall anyone of that name who lives around Tupelo. Elvis shrugs his shoulders and picks up a knife and fork, demonstrating that he is ready for his pancakes.

Does she know of any other Presleys in another part of Tennessee or Mississippi?

Minnie Mae frowns and begins to whistle, perhaps as an aid to concentration, before mentioning that Grandpappy Hood used to tell of a branch of the Presleys that lived in the backwoods around Fayette in Mississippi. She's never met them and, of course, it might be an old hillbilly story that has somehow became part of the family history.

But according to Grandpappy Hood, they had a big turnip patch and mainly lived on turnips – boiled, fried, mashed, roasted, any which way you can cook them.

"One other thing ah do remember him a-sayin.," adds Minnie Mae as she heaps the pancakes on to Elvis's plate. "Mind this might jest be another story, but he reckoned you'se could allus tell a Fayette Presley cus their ears stick out like jug handles."

Bubba tells Colonel Parker that there's a phone call for him from the Memphis Chief of Police. "You say you've got a Presley in the cells," replies the Colonel. "Well, it isn't Elvis because he's here with me. It's who? And he says his name is Eli and he's related to Elvis. Okay, Chief, thanks for letting us know. You're sorry, but you had no choice. I understand. We'll be right down to sort it out."

The Police Chief explains that they had to arrest him because of a disturbance in Beale Street that was threatening to turn into a small riot. The guy calling himself Eli Presley was in a pay phone booth and refusing to leave it even though he had been there for a couple of days. As an insurance he had chained himself inside the booth, claiming he was staying there because he was expecting a call from Elvis.

A crowd quickly built up of angry people wanting to use the phone, reinforcing their demands with shouts, and banging their fists against the booth.

Once word got out what was happening the crowd was swelled by sightseers interested in watching how the stand-off would end, while others turned up saying they wanted to be there to witness someone take a call from no less than the King, Elvis himself.

The result was a lot of pushing, shoving and punches being thrown, so the police had to move in.

Colonel Parker hands an envelope to the Police Chief, saying that Elvis insists on making a donation to the local police welfare fund, a cause very close to his heart, in recognition of the discreet way in which the whole situation has been handled.

"Why, Colonel, this isn't necessary," says the Police Chief, nevertheless feeling the thickness of the envelope before popping it into his pocket. "Please assure Elvis it will do a lot of good, and I believe I can say there's no need to take this matter any further."

When the Colonel sees Cousin Eli walking out of the cells, his heart sinks; not because he is wearing frayed, mud-stained dungarees and heavy boots, only one of which has a lace, but because his ears stick out from the side of his head like jug handles. If he were to walk into a strong headwind he'd take off like an aeroplane. There's no doubt about it, it's just like Minnie Mae says: he's a Fayette Presley.

"See how yer like this, Cousin Eli," says Minnie Mae as she hands him his dinner of squirrel fricassee, sweet potato mash and onion gravy.

"Gravy, oh my! Wut a treat! An' jest wut be these in this here dish, Miss Presley?"

"You be kinfolk so you'se can call me Minnie Mae. An' them there be deep-fried chitlins fritters. An' if'n yer can manage 'em, ah dun made some corn dodgers."

"Oooweee! This be a rare ole feast. It's jest like Christmas Day exceptin' there ain't no turnips. Wait till ah tell 'em back home. They ain't gonna believe it. Chitlins fritters! Whatever next!" He shakes his head in wonderment.

Priscilla questions if, back home in Fayette, they have ever tried something different like, for example, turnip mashed with swede and black-eyed peas to make their meals a bit more interesting.

"He he he," laughs Eli. "Wut an' spoil a perfectly good turnip!"

Elvis asks Eli what brings him to Memphis to see him. Eli's face clouds over as he tells them of a visit they'd received from some big shot lawyers from Jackson who told them about plans to build a battery chicken farm on their turnip patch.

"They say we ain't got no title ter the land an' we got ninety days ter find proof that we own it or we gotta come up with seventy-five thousand dollars ter buy it. Jest imagine – we gotta buy our own land! If'n we don't they'se gonna plough in our crop and start a-buildin' the chicken huts. Presleys have bin a-workin' that land fer generations, since afore the Secession of the South. Ah surely do declare, it jest ain't right."

"This be a cryin' shame an' a scandal," declares Minnie Mae. "Elvis, they be our kinfolk an' we surely gotta help."

Elvis frowns in concentration and fiddles with the fringes of his jumpsuit as he tries to think of a plan.

It is Cousin Eli himself who comes up with the answer. He is one of the lucky ones in the parish who has a radio and has heard Elvis sing. "We had a meetin' an' thought that if'n we could make a record with Elvis then mebbe we'd git a big enough pot of money ter buy our land."

Colonel Parker, once he has stopped slapping his thigh and hooting with laughter, points out that Elvis is not be allowed to make a record under his own name unless it is with RCA. His contract is tighter than a clam.

"But there isn't anything to stop us putting out a record by, say, the Turnip Boys on another label," counters Elvis, who's much taken with the idea. His involvement would have to be kept secret, of course, but if the record is good enough and with a bit of a push to promote it, it could sell and make some money.

A small recording studio is set up in the Jungle Room and Elvis, Eli and Charlie Hodge, Elvis's old friend and chief gofer, run through a few songs to get used to playing together. Because Elvis's voice is so distinctive, they decide that he and Charlie should do the backing vocals, with Eli taking the lead.

"Ah do declare ah'm a-makin' a record with Elvis an' ah'm as happy as a boll weevil in a field o' cotton," beams Eli. "Y'all can bear witness that the age o' miracles ain't dun yet."

Folks back in Fayette want him to record Miles and Bob Pratcher's *All Night Long* because they come to play every year at the annual turnip festival, and it's a good old country jig. As well as singing Eli also plays fiddle and jug. For the B side they choose Roy Acuff's *The Great Speckled Bird*.

"Do you have a Turnip Queen at the festival?" wonders Charlie.

"Why we surely do!" responds Eli. "If'n it's a tie the winner is the gal with the most teeth."

The record is released on the Hi label and within a week it is a hit in Memphis – thanks to a 'nod and a wink' call that Elvis makes to his old school friend and DJ George Klein at Radio WHBQ.

George tells his listeners: "I'm going to play this new record by the Turnip Boys and then I'm going to ask you a question, so listen very carefully."

Afterwards he says: "What a great record that is and I'm tipping it for the top. I don't know about you, but I can hear somebody who sounds like Elvis doing the back-up vocals. We go back a long way, Elvis and me; we were at Humes High School together. Of course, I know it can't really be him, but it is an uncanny likeness. I'm going to play it again and I want you to call me here on my 'Talent Party' show on WHBQ and tell me what you think."

A week later the record is a huge hit across Tennessee, Mississippi, Kentucky, and Arkansas. Elvis fans are buying it because it might be him who's singing, Rufus Thomas has introduced a turnip dance, and newspapers are reporting that girls are taking turnips to clubs and dance halls and dancing around them instead of their handbags.

Sales of the record easily surpass the $75,000 needed to buy the turnip patch and there is plenty left to acquire some adjacent land where they can plant even more turnips.

In revenge for attempting to throw Eli and the other Presleys off their land they decide to delay the announcement of their success until the very last moment, in order to cause the maximum inconvenience, expense and embarrassment to the big shot lawyers from Jackson.

A convoy of men, trucks, tractors and cranes draws up to the turnip patch out in the backwoods near Fayette, ready to start work on building the battery chicken farm, only to find themselves confronted by Eli and two guys in grey suits and steel-framed spectacles.

"Ah'm a-warnin' y'all not to enter my property," declares Eli. "Or you're gonna be real sorry."

It takes a while for the driver of the lead truck to stop laughing. He opens up the CB channel and says over the radio to the rest of the convoy: "This is the Rubber Duck and my day has just got better. This guy who is trying to stop us is a comedian as well as a turnip farmer. He's funnier than Rodney Dangerfield; he should be on TV. Okay, I'm gonna power up, so follow me and let's roll, ten-four."

As he starts to move forward the two men in grey suits step in front of the truck. What the foreman doesn't know is that they are senior counsel from Shyster & Shyster, a New York firm of lawyers used by Colonel Parker.

One of them waves a piece of paper and says: "This affidavit confirms that seventy-five thousand dollars was paid earlier today by the Bank of Jefferson Davis to secure ownership of this land in perpetuity. Mr Eli Presley is now the owner and you and your truck are trespassing on his property. He is perfectly within his rights to open fire, but instead I expect he will be guided by us to sue you for trespass, damage to his land and its restitution, and distress to his feelings."

The lead trucker looks at the piece of paper; it's mumbo jumbo as far as he is concerned, full of fancy long words he doesn't understand. And who is to say that it is genuine or that these two guys are who they say they are? He keeps the engine revving while he considers how long it has taken them to get there from Jackson and the fact that if they don't start work, they don't get paid.

"What the hell!" he declares, jams his foot on the accelerator and his truck rolls forward, causing the two lawyers to leap out of the way.

At that moment he sees Elvis step from a car parked in the middle of the field. There is no mistaking who it is, dressed in his famous sunburst jumpsuit, airline pilot sunglasses and jet-black hair.

Elvis always suspected that he'd be needed and that the presence of the two lawyers from Shyster & Shyster would not be enough.

He adopts a John Wayne walk as he makes his way to the truck and says, "I'm sorry but I'd be much obliged if you guys would all turn round and go home. These are my kinfolk, and they legally own the land. You have seen the affidavit from the lawyers. Please do this for me and my folks."

The leader of the convoy is back on the CB radio. "This is the Rubber Duck. You won't believe this but I'm talking to Elvis. Repeat I am talking to Elvis! The King! Ten-four." Word spreads like wildfire through the convoy. All the drivers climb out of their cabs to huddle round him and shake his hand. They all agree: if this is what Elvis wants, that's what they'll do.

The leader of the convoy raises his arm in the air. "Look, it's the hand that shook the hand of Elvis. I can't wait to get back home and tell my wife and kids!"

The drivers climb back in their cabs and the convoy turns round and heads back towards Jackson, horns tooting in a tribute to Elvis.

A few days later he and the Colonel are invited back so that Eli and his Presley kinfolk can say thank you for all that they have done for them. They arrive to find that benches have been set out among the apple trees in the orchard for a celebration lunch.

"Lordy, y'all must be a-starvin' after a-comin' all the way from Memphis," says Eli, who is wearing new dungarees and boots. Things must be looking up for them, Elvis is pleased to see.

Colonel Parker already has indigestion brought on by fear; he is worried that what he is about to eat will make Minnie Mae look like a Cordon Bleu chef. He'd reluctantly agreed to make the trip on condition that they were back at Graceland that same evening, meaning he only has to endure one meal. However, he reminds himself that this branch of the family are undoubtedly Presleys and, therefore, he must do his duty. But thank goodness, Elvis didn't inherit their jug ears – it would have finished his career.

They're introduced to Cousin Doug who, they're told, has appeared in a movie. He is concentrating hard on cleaning his fingernails with the tip of a big hunting knife which he waves in their direction before returning to his manicure.

Elvis is naturally curious that another Presley has made a film.

Cousin Doug, known as Mad Dog, was in the movie *Deliverance* as one of the mountain men who hunt the four businessmen on their canoe trip down a river in the wilds of Georgia.

He takes a shine to the character played by Ned Beatty, is how Eli explains his role as delicately as possible. The director said he was a born actor, and all he had to do was be himself.

"Listen up, people. We gotta let our guests fill their plates first," announces Eli, as a huge pie is placed in the centre of the table. With a bunch of green leaves sprouting from the crust, Elvis doesn't need to ask what sort of pie it is.

A young girl walks over to the Colonel and smiles as she looks him over; noting his size, she calls for an extra-large helping. Similarly, he can tell from the number of teeth in her mouth that she was never the Turnip Queen.

A toast is drunk with a spirit distilled from turnips. Elvis takes a sip, and it feels like he is drinking fire. What damage might it do to his throat? He surreptitiously empties the contents of the glass on to the grass at his feet and watches as it immediately shrivels and turns brown.

Unluckily, a cousin notices his empty glass. "Well ah do declare," he calls out. "Lookee here! Elvis dun got a taste fer our liquor. Git him a bigger glass an' give him a refill. Y'all can tell he ain't never forgot his country roots."

In his speech of thanks Cousin Eli says that they've had a meeting about what to do with the money that's left over from the record sales now that they have bought the land. After discussing a number of ideas they've decided to invest in a new variety that will yield bigger and juicier turnips.

"Folks here be already a-lickin' their lips," he says.

Elvis and Colonel Parker are invited to stay for supper and the hoedown, but they apologise, saying that they must hurry back to Memphis for important business meetings. As far as the Colonel is concerned, he hopes it will be a long time before he becomes reacquainted with the Fayette Presleys and their turnip patch.

As he and Elvis return to the car, pleased to be making their escape, Eli runs up and clamps his hands on their shoulders as he walks between them. He points out that the future for the Fayette Presleys may not depend solely upon turnips, and that new opportunities are opening up for them in the field of entertainment.

That's good to hear, comments Elvis, while icy fingers clutch his manager's heart as he dreads being asked to manage them.

"Mad Dog Doug is a-hopin' fer a part in another film," he continues, "an' folks here are a-tellin' me wut a mighty fine singing voice ah've got. So ah'm a-wonderin' if'n ah can ask fer one more small favour?

"Ah've bin a-learnin' a new song an' ah'd be much obliged ter come ter Graceland agin an' make a new record."

THE TUPELO THUNDERBOLT

Priscilla and Minnie Mae are looking out of the kitchen window when they see a horsebox come up the drive and park outside the front of Graceland. They watch a man in a brown waistcoat, jodhpurs and riding boots lead out a horse; he ties the reins around the neck of one of the stone lions at the foot of the steps, tucks a letter under the bridle, and then drives off.

They look quizzically at each other.

"Has Elvis said anything to you about this?" asks Priscilla. Minnie Mae shakes her head. At various times Elvis has been known to turn up at Graceland with pets such as a peacock, a goat, and a chimpanzee, so a horse may not come as such a complete surprise.

"Do you know, I think it might be a racehorse," says Priscilla, peering intently through the window. "Look at the saddle and the cloth underneath with the big number thirteen on it."

Minnie Mae tells her: "It surely don't look like one o' them ole nags that Grandpappy Hood dun used ter pull a plough out in the fields. It be too scrawny."

"Is it for Elvis's next movie?" wonders Priscilla. "I've not heard anything, but it could be for the two of them to get to know each other before filming starts. Perhaps it's going to be a western, but he always said he'd never do another one after *Charro!*"

Minnie Mae starts to chuckle. "Well ah do declare that horse already be a-feelin' right at home."

"Yes, I can see how relaxed he is. I'll tell Charlie to get a shovel and a bucket."

"An' tell him to put it around the roses."

When Minnie Mae says she needs to start skinning the squirrels for that evening's fricassee, Priscilla decides it is a good time to leave the kitchen and go and see Elvis and Colonel Parker to find out what is going on.

A meeting is called in the dining room to try and discover how a racehorse came to be delivered to Graceland. According to the documents left with it, it is now owned by Elvis and its name – the previous one having been scribbled out – is the Tupelo Thunderbolt.

"Daddy, does this have anything to do with that race meeting you went to at Churchill Downs in Kentucky with Jerry Lee Lewis?" asks Elvis. "I know how he likes to take a walk down the wild side of life. You weren't drinking, were you?"

Vernon looks shamefaced as he slowly rotates the brim of his Stetson hat in his hands. "Maybe just one or two – nothing more. It was a warm day."

Elvis sighs and ruefully shakes his head. Vernon has form, having returned once before from a night out with Jerry Lee, believing he'd bought a share in the Peabody Hotel in Memphis. "Tell us what happened, Daddy."

Vernon recounts how, after the last race, they had left the hospitality suite to go home and had got as far as the parade ring. "I remember somebody calling out, 'Is there anybody here from Tennessee?' Jerry Lee nudged me, so I put up my hand. When this guy asked me what the time was, I looked at my watch and said, 'Five.' Of course, I meant it was five o'clock. But the next thing I know he's shouting 'Sold!' He came over, thumped me on the back, and congratulated me on buying a racehorse for five thousand dollars.

"Ole Jerry Lee was laughing like a hyena that was being tickled. The guy told me I was making a brilliant investment, one that would make my fortune. 'You spotted it straight away, didn't you,' he said. 'What?' I replied. 'That this horse you've just bought is a son of the legendary Seabiscuit, America's greatest racehorse. You've got the eye. By the way, who should I make out the invoice to, and where should I send the horse?' I was flummoxed, in a daze, not knowing what to do. I must have said 'Elvis' and 'Graceland' without thinking. I'm sorry son."

There's a buzz of excitement in the room. Even Red and Sonny West, who only read the funny papers, have heard of Seabiscuit and what a great racehorse he was. "He always won and, it stands to reason, like father, like son," they whisper to each other. "It figures that the Tupelo Thunderbolt must be a winner as well. We'll bet big on every race, and we'll clean up. Oh boy, we're gonna be rich!" The cousins grin and shake each other by the hand.

"Whoa! Hold your horses!" shouts Colonel Parker, trying to quell the hubbub. "First, we need to make sure this horse really is a son of Seabiscuit." He asks his assistant, Bubba, to go and make some enquiries.

He puts on a sorrowful expression, wrings his hands, and says, "I don't want to put a damper on the party, but do you have any idea how much it costs to own a racehorse?" He pushes back his straw trilby and mops his brow. The thought of the steady ebb and flow of big-number invoices and the serious amounts of money that will be spent on a horse is causing him to overheat.

"I'm no expert but there's the trainer, the stables, the vets' bills, the special diet of hay and grain, the entry fees for races... I'm sorry, folks, the whole thing is making me feel faint. We must be realistic about how expensive it will be – a huge drag on the Graceland budget."

Elvis surveys the dejected faces around the room. The excitement at the possibility that Vernon might have bought a racehorse sired by the legendary Seabiscuit has subsided into the silence of disappointment. Yes, he concedes, the odds may be 1,000 to 1 against it being true. Yes, it probably is a pipe dream, and a lovely one at that, but should his manager be allowed to kill it at birth?

He mulls it over in his mind and thinks that there may be a way to keep the dream alive and have some fun along the way.

"No!" Elvis calls out. "I say we can do it!"

This shock announcement makes Colonel Parker's jaw drop so quickly in astonishment that his chins begin to wobble. "Madness!" he splutters.

But he soon cheers up as Elvis explains how looking after and training the Tupelo Thunderbolt can be done right here at Graceland, and there is no need to look beyond the Music Gates for assistance.

"He'll be kept in the stables with the other horses and Vernon will groom him. And that includes mucking-out."

"That ain't fair, son. I call that housework and that's Charlie's job."

"I'm sorry, Daddy, but I've got something else in mind for Charlie, and don't forget who it was that bought the racehorse."

He continues: "Minnie Mae, you'll be in charge of his diet."

There is a gallery of appalled faces around the room as they reflect on the kind of meals she prepares for them, such as squirrel fricassee, catfish stew and deep-fried battered chitlins, and they wonder what might end up in the poor thing's nosebag.

Sensing the unease, Elvis assures them: "Dodger was born and raised on a farm. Nobody knows better than she does what to feed a horse. He'll fine dine like a king on the very best hay and oats."

"But they were old nags that pulled a plough on her farm, not thoroughbreds!" states Lamar Fike to knowing nods from the others.

"Don't be a-feared," she tells them. "Ah'm a-gonna have him a-flyin' faster than that white horse with wings, the one that wus called Peggy Sue."

Elvis asks Dr Nick, his personal physician, if he is also a qualified vet. He frowns and strokes his chin and says he can't remember. He has more than 20 medical qualifications, obtained from correspondence courses with the University of Swampwater, which are displayed on a wall in his office-cum-pharmacy.

"It's very likely, but I'll need to check just to be sure," he answers. "If not, I'll enrol for one of their courses."

Elvis concludes by saying that once a day he or Priscilla will ride the racehorse around the grounds of Graceland to build up his stamina and speed.

"But what about me, Elvis?" cries Charlie. "You said you had a job for me."

"Yes, Charlie, and it is a very important one. We need somebody small and light to be his jockey when he races. And that's you!"

There is a tapping on the door and Bubba walks in and apologises, saying he has some bad news concerning the racehorse's pedigree. Seabiscuit was put out to stud in 1940 when he retired and died in 1947. That means that if the Tupelo Thunderbolt was sired by him, he's anything between 26 and 33 years old!

There is a chorus of groans and much shaking of heads, as they all wade together into the slough of despond.

"We should rename him Old Father Time," grumbles Red West.

"Or Methuselah," adds Sonny.

"Maybe we should put him in a bathchair and Charlie can push him around the course," sneers Lamar.

"Of course, there is one obvious explanation," declares Colonel Parker. "It's an old carny trick." He pauses to puff on his cigar to build up the suspense among his listeners, before telling them: "I believe it's a deadbeat hack that was palmed off on an unsuspecting patsy, namely Vernon."

Priscilla sighs. "It was a nice dream while it lasted. Let's get back to reality."

As they begin to file out of the room Elvis calls out: "Hold on, everybody. There's one other possibility. What if they've made a mistake, and the Tupelo Thunderbolt is not the son, but the great-great- great- great-grandson of Seabiscuit. There's one sure way we can find out how good he is. And that, my friends, is because we're gonna go racing."

The announcement ignites a party atmosphere and a bout of congratulations and handshaking as they all leave the room. Colonel Parker remains in his seat, inscrutable.

"I see they've ignored your words of wisdom, sir," comments Bubba. "Such folly. What do we do now?"

"We're going to treat this racehorse business like we do any other Elvis event," he replies, "and we'll publicise it and merchandise it to death and not worry about whether it'll win. Let's get back to the office and start making plans."

Within a week, stories planted by the Colonel begin to appear on TV and in the newspapers about the Tupelo Thunderbolt, accompanied by pictures of Elvis riding him in the grounds of Graceland. There is even an article on the front page of the Wall Street Journal, headlined 'The Elvis Effect' that speculates on the millions of dollars that will flow into the sport of horseracing as a result of Elvis's involvement.

While racecourse owners rub their hands with glee at the prospect of the vast crowds that will turn up to see Elvis and his horse run, bookmakers are terrified. How many of his many millions of fans will bet on it? Possibly every one of them. The Tupelo Thunderbolt might as well race as one of the Four Horsemen of the Apocalypse because, if he should win, the scale of the pay-out would wipe out many of the bookmakers.

Features appear spread over several pages in Women's Wear Daily and Vogue on Priscilla and the outfits she will wear when she goes racing. Edith Head, the top Hollywood designer, and Dior reveal that they are hard at work on a wardrobe of haute couture designs.

By popular demand, so he says, Colonel Parker has launched the Tupelo Thunderbolt Fan Club, with membership priced at $20 to cover administration and the production and postage of a regular newsletter. A lottery is launched, exclusive to fan club members, who, for $10, can enter a draw to find four winners who will each have their name engraved on a horseshoe to be used by the horse in his first race.

Statuettes of the racehorse made from recyclable plastic can also be purchased for $25, although some critics point out their similarity to Roy Rogers' horse, Trigger, particularly the saddle, which is like the ones used by cowboys not horse racing jockeys.

Elvis is puzzled as he stands, stopwatch and clipboard in hand, as the Tupelo Thunderbolt saunters past the finishing post on the small training course that has been set up in the grounds at Graceland. Despite the urgings of Charlie, his jockey, his times never get any quicker. It is a mystery, because he looks to be in peak condition; his coat gleams like polished rosewood, and Vernon has confirmed to Dr Nick that he eats well and is definitely not constipated.

"What is it we're not doing?" he confides to Priscilla, who is standing next to him. "What can we do to get him to go faster? Should I ask Minnie Mae to change his diet?"

"No, don't do that, Elvis, she could set him back for weeks. I have a theory that he's smarter than you think. I believe he is saving himself for the day of the race; when he gets out on the course, hears the noise of the crowd and lines up with the other racehorses, then his ears will prick up, he'll come alive, and we'll see the real Tupelo Thunderbolt. It's what a lot of top athletes do – they don't overtrain but save themselves for one explosive effort when it really matters in the race."

He asks her: "You think we should enter him in a race and see what happens?"

"Yes, I do."

Swelled by fans who've come to see Elvis and his racehorse, the crowds at the Churchill Downs course are much bigger than even those that attend the annual Kentucky Derby, the USA's most famous race. There was disappointment at Graceland when Elvis ruled against entering the Tupelo Thunderbolt in such a prestigious event. He explained that he didn't want to put too much pressure on the horse or the jockey, Charlie Hodge, so he entered him in the Mason Dixon Stakes, a one-and-a-half-mile handicap.

His fans begin chanting 'Elvis! Elvis!' as soon as he steps into the parade ring, dressed conservatively in the purple suit that he wore on the famous occasion when he met President Nixon in the White House. Priscilla is wearing a pink woollen suit with a white silk blouse and white gloves, these being the Presley racing colours. Being quite small she insisted on wearing very high, thin stiletto shoes, which sink into the turf like tent pegs.

While Elvis walks across to the fans who continue to call out his name, Priscilla has to stay where she is.

He tells them: "Thank you. I 'Can't Help Falling in Love' with you all."

The stewards and police officers are struggling to hold back his fans as they surge forward, desperate to reach out and touch him. Elvis raises an arm and urges them to calm down and a voice at the back shouts: "The King has spoken." Immediately, there is silence, and the crowd is as quiet and orderly as if they were attending a church service.

The other racehorse owners in the parade ring, with the men in morning suits and top hats and the ladies in floral dresses, mink wraps and big hats, are appalled at what is happening; Elvis is turning the race meeting into something akin to a rock concert. They stay together in a huddle on the other side of the parade ring, as far away as possible from him and his party, and where they can tut-tut without being overheard. Although they won't admit it, they're grateful, nevertheless, for the crowds and, correspondingly, the money that he has attracted to the course.

It is cloudy with a slight chill in the air, causing Priscilla to shiver.

"We're in Kentucky an' the weather be as uncertain as a babe's bottom," declares Minnie Mae, who is dressed for the occasion in new dungarees, lace-up boots and a soft felt cloche hat, with a plastic flower attached.

"Pay it no mind, Priscilla, cus mah big toe is a-tellin' me that sunshine be a-comin' soon. You'se can allus rely on mah toe."

The horses that will run in the Mason Dixon Stakes enter the ring, with the Tupelo Thunderbolt led by Vernon, still to be reconciled with being called head lad. "It ain't right," he complains to Elvis. "Folks will laugh themselves silly. I'm a grandfather – not a boy!"

"It's just the traditional name they use, Daddy," he says, trying to placate him.

Now the jockeys walk into the parade ring.

Bernard Lansky, who has designed most of Elvis's outfits since his days at Sun, has promised that everybody will be able to spot Elvis's horse in the race, even when it is at the furthest point from the grandstand. He is as good as his word. Charlie's racing colours include a pink shirt with, on the chest, an image of a finishing post picked out in red and white rhinestones and, on the back, there's a large image of the Tupelo Thunderbolt's head in silver sequins and crystals. His white cap is covered in rhinestones with the initials EP in pink; a white cape features a large image of Graceland in silver sequins and, instead of the usual jodhpurs, he is wearing white flared trousers with crystals along the seams. He looks as if he has arrived from having performed at one of Elvis's shows in Las Vegas.

The other jockeys, who've joined the owners on the far side of the parade ring, smirk and snigger and point at him with their whips.

Word has reached the bookmakers, who cannot believe their luck. Not only has Elvis entered a perpetual loser, but he is being ridden by a clown. There is no way this horse can win. In the history of hopeless causes, goes the joke circulating among the bookies, this one must take the Seabiscuit. They lengthen the odds on the Tupelo Thunderbolt to attract more bets from the suckers who want to put money on a horse owned by Elvis. They are still laughing as the announcement is made for the horses to make their way to the start.

"Any advice for me, Elvis?" asks Charlie. "What should I do?"

Elvis ponders a moment or two before telling him: "Don't fall off."

As the horses are being put into the stalls at the start, just as Minnie Mae predicted, the sun bursts from behind the clouds, bringing with it a quickly spreading blue sky.

The stalls open but one only one racehorse heads up the course, albeit not very quickly – the Tupelo Thunderbolt. Behind him there is chaos. The sun has turned Charlie, whose racing outfit is covered in thousands of rhinestones, crystals, and sequins, into a dazzling blaze of white light that blinds the other horses. In their terror, they rear up and kick out, and the jockeys fight with the reins to stop them charging off in the opposite direction.

Meanwhile, the Tupelo Thunderbolt continues at a pace somewhere between a trot and a steady gallop. Once he has rounded the bend and is out of sight, the jockeys manage to regain control of their mounts who are no longer dazzled and set off in pursuit.

By now the Tupelo Thunderbolt is in the home straight, but the other horses are gaining fast. Elvis, Priscilla (who has left her shoes where they were held fast in the ground), Minnie Mae and Vernon have run to stand by the finishing post, yelling at him to go faster.

As the rest of the field come round the bend, they are once again confronted by the dazzling brilliance of Charlie, as if they are running towards the sun.

They might have stood a chance if they'd been racing in sunglasses but, blinded again, they come to a sudden stop. The jockeys' shouts of frustration can be heard from the stands, but the horses refuse to do more than trot round in confused circles, as if they were performing a barn dance.

The Tupelo Thunderbolt crosses the finishing line and is judged to have won by 50 lengths.

Charlie rides into the winner's enclosure to cheers from the crowd, doubly delighted that Elvis's horse has won, and that they'd put a bet on him. And so, it transpires, has everybody at Graceland – with one exception, the man addicted to gambling. Colonel Parker carefully examined the horse's pedigree, form, training, diet, and jockey, came to the obvious conclusion that there was no way it could possibly win. Consequently, he'd bet heavily against it. And lost.

"We did it, King!" shouts Charlie excitedly. "We've won! The Thunderbolt must have been racing like the wind because the other horses never got near us once we left the start. He was just too fast for them – they couldn't catch us."

"I don't know how you did it," laughs Elvis.

They are besieged by reporters and TV crews who want pictures of Elvis, Priscilla, Minnie Mae, Vernon, and Charlie with the Tupelo Thunderbolt. "How did you turn a horse that had never won before into a winner?" they ask Elvis. (The headlines next day describe it as 'The greatest comeback since Lazarus'.)

"What's your secret?" they want to know. "Here they are," he replies, and tells Priscilla, Vernon, Minnie Mae, and Charlie to step forward and take a bow.

They bombard him with questions: "Will you train more horses? Will you use your magic to turn other no-hopers into winners? What about rock and roll and the movies, or is this going to be your future?"

Elvis's response is an enigmatic smile and a wave as they walk away for the presentation to the owners of the winner of the Mason Dixon Stakes.

Meanwhile, the stewards and police have been diverted to control the thousands of people milling around the bookmakers, trying to collect their winnings. They are also there to ensure that the bookies don't try and make a run for it.

A short while later rumours begin to circulate of a secret meeting that takes place between the trade body representing horseracing bookmakers and Elvis.

Although it is emphatically denied that such a thing happened, three representatives go to Graceland for talks with Elvis and his manager. They walk into Colonel Parker's office waving a small white flag, begging for mercy. All it would take, they say, is for one more race to be won by the Tupelo Thunderbolt, with bets placed on him by millions of Elvis fans, to wipe out the bookmaking business.

They offer half a million dollars to buy him with the promise to place him with the Life of Riley stud farm in Kentucky where he can happily live out his days.

Elvis protests: "No, no, no. He's full of life, he loves racing, and you want to retire him years before his time."

"It's a stud farm," they point out. "He'll be kept busy and be very happy."

Colonel Parker doesn't bat an eyelid at the mention of half a million dollars. He is like a cat that has cornered three mice; he has all the time in the world to toy with them because there is no way they can escape. It's time to make his opening gambit.

"This horse was born to race – and win," he declares. "The Great American Public are urging Elvis to announce his next race; we're thinking of perhaps the Belmont Stakes or the Santa Anita Derby."

There is a deep, heartfelt groan from the bookmakers' representatives. "It would ruin us," they respond, with another wave of the white flag.

The Colonel continues to puff on his cigar, seemingly deep in thought, before announcing: "Elvis and I have been talking to a business associate of ours about the future of the Tupelo Thunderbolt." This is news that comes as a complete surprise to Elvis. It also unnerves the bookmakers' representatives.

He continues: "Let's start by dismissing this nonsense concerning half a million dollars. But for two million dollars you will be making an investment that will secure the horse's future as well as keeping him away from racecourses. What's more, the project I have in mind will make a lot of money for yourselves and Elvis. Trust me, it's a win-win."

"Two million dollars, you say," reply the bookmakers' representatives.

"Yes, but that doesn't include my fee."

They look at each other. All they'd been told beforehand about Colonel Parker is true.

They take a deep breath and steel themselves for the worst. "Okay, tell us about this scheme."

A few weeks later a press conference is held in a marquee set up in the grounds of Graceland for an important briefing on the future of The Tupelo Thunderbolt. The TV crews and reporters arrive, expecting to be told what his next race will be; perhaps, and this would be sensational news, he'll go for the Triple Crown.

They are stunned when Elvis announces, to a script prepared by the Colonel: "I know that a new star of horse racing was born when The Tupelo Thunderbolt won the Mason Dixon Stakes by such a history-making distance. Who knows what other triumphs he could have gone on to achieve. Racegoers have taken him to their hearts. But a wonderful new opportunity has come his way and I hope that all his supporters will agree that it is the best thing that could happen for him and horse racing in general."

He reveals that The Tupelo Thunderbolt is to star in a movie produced by Hal Wallis, the producer of many of his own films. Afterwards he will retire to stud to sire many more champions. Elvis leads the applause as the Tupelo Thunderbolt is led into the marquee by his head lad, Vernon, accompanied by Hal Wallis.

Shots are taken of Elvis and Hal standing alongside the racehorse, and then comes Colonel Parker's big idea, one right out of the carny handbook. The Tupelo Thunderbolt is led forward to sign the contract by stepping on it and making the imprint of a horseshoe.

Understandably, the media want to know about the film, as do the representatives of the bookmakers' trade organisation, given the size of their investment in the project. They will also be pressing the Colonel later about the size of the stud fees and how they'll be shared.

Hal says that the script is still in development, but the movie will focus on the Cinderella story of how the Tupelo Thunderbolt was transformed from an also-ran into a champion by Elvis and his team at Graceland.

A barrage of questions is fired at him about who will star in the movie. "These are early days, but obviously, there's nobody who can play Elvis but Elvis," he declares, but refuses to answer any more questions, saying they'll have to wait and see.

Some months later, Elvis and Priscilla are sitting in their home in Beverley Hills, having attended the Hollywood premiere of the movie about the Tupelo Thunderbolt the previous evening.

She asks him: "Tell me, honestly, Elvis, what did you think of it?"

"It was good, but I don't think it will win any Oscars."

"I don't think it was good. In fact, I reckon it was a failure. And do you know what I think the problem is? Apart from you, everybody else involved with the story is played by actors, including me! It doesn't have that ring of truth that we'd bring to it. I mean, Ann-Margret was nothing like the real me. Whose idea was it to cast her because it was a big mistake?"

Elvis can feel himself blushing and begins to cough violently to cover up. He's finally able to tell her that it was Hal Wallis's decision, based on how well they'd worked together on *Viva Las Vegas*.

"You have to remember, honey, there was a very small window of time available to shoot the movie," he explains. "That meant Hal had to use professional actors. Even the Tupelo Thunderbolt is played by a professional, union-card-holding horse. That's the movie business for you!"

A TSUNAMI OF ELVISES

It is the climax of another show at the Las Vegas International. Elvis finishes *Can't Help Falling in Love* and, with a final wave to his fans, he leaves the stage followed by Charlie Hodge, his old friend and faithful gofer.

After Charlie has handed him a towel to wrap around his neck and another one to mop his face, Elvis sets off down the long ramp towards the limousine, waiting with its engine running; Charlie, who is a lot shorter, runs to keep up with him.

He opens a door at the rear of the car and gives another towel to Elvis who looks as if he has just stepped out of a sauna. On the seat is a large bottle of Coke, most of which he drains in one go, and a flat box the size of a kitchen table.

"It's the Everest meat feast pizza," Charlie informs him.

"Deep fried?"

"Yes, just as you like it, King."

In terms of the time it takes, it would be quicker for Elvis to walk to his suite at the International Hotel. But the routine of how he ends each performance by running off stage and climbing into a limousine with its engine running has become as much an iconic part of the show as the opening with its fanfare of *2001: A Space Odyssey* which segues into *C C Rider*. Consequently, the limousine will drive around the block before pulling up at a side entrance with access to a private lift to Elvis's suite.

He tucks into the pizza while the engine ticks over until they hear the announcement. "Ladies and Gentlemen, Elvis has left the building." He taps the partition glass, and the car accelerates away.

Elvis asks him what he thought of the show. "Fantastic!" responds Charlie. "I believe it was one of your very best. Ever!"

"Ah," says Charlie, seeing a picture of a hippopotamus advertising a wildlife park, as they drive by, "that reminds me. Colonel Parker asked me to give you this at the end of the show."

He hands him an envelope which Elvis opens to find another envelope inside with 'Top Secret' written on it. He opens it and reads it.

"What does it say?" inquires Charlie.

"Colonel Parker wants to see me tomorrow about an exciting new business venture that will revolutionise our merchandising. It is so secret that I'm to tell absolutely nobody about it."

"But you've just told me."

"Oops, in which case you'd better eat this note. I've seen it on TV. It's what they always do in cases like this."

"But, Elvis…" whinges Charlie, but Elvis is implacable.

He returns to eating his Everest meat feast pizza while Charlie rips up the note and starts to chew the first piece.

"And forget what I told you about the meeting," Elvis tells him.

"Forget what?"

"Exactly."

Next day Elvis knocks on the door of his manager's office in Graceland.

"Who's there?" he hears Colonel Parker say.

"Elvis. You asked me to come to a meeting in your office."

"Is there anybody else there with you?"

"No."

"Come in quickly and lock the door behind you."

Once Elvis is seated, he nods to Bubba, his assistant, who goes and stuffs tissue paper into the lock.

Elvis looks mystified at what is going on, but the Colonel explains: "I don't want any ears flapping next to the keyhole and hearing what we're discussing. Son, this is big. Bigger than big. It's monumental."

He suddenly spins round in his chair as if trying to catch somebody standing behind him. "You cannot be too careful," he declares, tapping the side of his nose with his cigar. "Security has to be tighter than Jack Benny's wallet."

He bends down and produces a black leather briefcase, and from around his neck, he removes a loop of string with a key tied to it; Bubba does the same with another key, and together they each open one of the spring locks.

The Colonel looks at something inked on the palm of his hand

and tells Bubba to open the tumbler lock on the briefcase using the numbers 1-8-35.

"Hey, what a coincidence. That's the date of my birthday!" exclaims Elvis cheerily.

"That's right, son! That's how the good ole Colonel fools them every time! They'll think I'll use my own birthday for the code. I'm too smart for them because I've used the date of your birthday instead!"

He chortles to himself, so pleased with his ingenuity. He is on a roll and takes a pull at the lever of the gaming machine that he keeps next to his desk, but once again, he loses. He shrugs philosophically, but for once he doesn't mind because there is a big winner inside the briefcase.

He recommends that Elvis should stand next to the desk. With a flourish, like a conjuror producing a rabbit from a hat, he opens the briefcase and then, gesturing with his cigar, invites him to take a look.

"Contain your excitement," he advises, "but be prepared to be amazed. You are going to be gazing at the future of merchandising."

Elvis leans forward and suddenly staggers back as if he has been bitten by a snake. "Hells bells, Colonel, sir! It's a voodoo doll!" he exclaims, pointing a shaky finger at the case. "Why are you messing with black magic?"

Colonel Parker laughs in a ho-ho-ho Father Christmas sort of way. "Now come on, son, and take another look."

Gingerly, he edges forward, crossing his fingers behind his back as he peeps into the briefcase. "Well, Colonel, sir, at least there aren't any pins sticking in the doll but it's still pretty scary."

His manager shakes his head sorrowfully and says, "Don't you recognise yourself, son. It's you!" The 18-inch-high doll has a mop of black hair and is dressed in a silvery jumpsuit with flared trousers and a short cape which the Colonel lifts to reveal a ring pull. He gives it a tug and the doll sings *C C Rider* in a mechanical voice with a trace of a Chinese accent.

Elvis is aghast. "Colonel, sir, it doesn't look like me and it sure as hell doesn't sound like me."

His manager urges him to stay calm, because what he is seeing and hearing is a er... er... "What is it, Bubba?"

"A prototype, sir."

"That's it. You have my word, Elvis, that these very small concerns of yours will be fixed. But you need to see the bigger picture. Let me explain."

"It's a devil doll," mutters Elvis under his breath.

The big picture is that the Colonel is planning to introduce a range of collectable Elvis dolls, starting with this Las Vegas version. There will be many more in the series such as the Jailhouse Rock doll, the Comeback Special white suit and black leather dolls, the Cowboy doll and the G.I. Blues doll.

He believes there will be a stampede of Elvis fans around the world who will want to collect the whole set, paying a very reasonable $25 a time. By some quirk in the manufacturing process, only a third of one of the dolls in the series will be manufactured; as a result, collectors will scramble not to miss out, and a bidding war will drive up the price even higher.

What Colonel Parker does not mention is that he has found a sweatshop in the Far East that can make them in the tens of thousands for about one dollar a doll. It's the granddaddy of all his merchandising schemes, one that is going to unleash a tsunami of dollars.

Bubba presses the doorbell that is shaped like a grand piano and the chimes play the opening bars of Mozart's *Eine Kleine Nachtmusik.* The door is opened by Brother George, dressed in a Jeeves-like gentleman's gentleman outfit. He nods by way of a greeting and beckons them to enter. "Please wait a moment while I announce you," he says solemnly.

Elvis, Colonel Parker, and Bubba have been invited to the Los Angeles home of Liberace to discuss his idea for a TV Special which he describes as 'sensational'.

The Colonel was sceptical about going, since he is the one who likes to take the lead with ideas about TV Specials. But Elvis is intrigued and so he begrudgingly relents, providing they can combine the trip with a meeting with producer Hal Wallis at Paramount studios. Apparently, he has a 15-day window becoming available in the near future, which would be long enough to shoot an Elvis movie. It's news that makes Elvis's heart sink – please let it not be another turkey like *Stay Away, Joe* – but he hopes for better things from the meeting with Liberace, his old friend and fellow Las Vegas superstar.

They find him resting on a lounger beside a piano-shaped swimming pool, holding a cocktail glass complete with straw, frilly paper umbrella and a stirrer that looks like a conductor's baton. The edges of the pool are decorated like the keys of a piano, and a conductor's rostrum acts as a diving platform.

While Brother George goes off to fetch nibbles for everyone, having first placed an antique rococo candelabrum on the table, they are joined by Liberace's mother, Frances.

"Elvis, I'm so excited," she declares, fluttering a hand in front of her face like a fan. "As soon as I heard it was you who'd arrived, I just had to come and say hello. I see you have brought two friends with you. Such a pity that Priscilla couldn't come too."

Elvis stands up to give her a hug and introduces the Colonel and Bubba.

"Isn't she as pretty as a picture?" smiles Liberace, raising his glass to toast her.

Courtesy requires Elvis to liken her to the Mona Lisa, knowing how devoted Liberace is to his mother, as indeed, he was to his own.

Her full-length pink, frothy dress with batwing sleeves covers everything apart from her wrinkled face and hands. Her white hair is pinned up and the ensemble is completed by her spectacles that are decorated with what are probably diamonds rather than diamante.

"That nice Mr Dior flew over here in a private jet to personally deliver this dress," she tells him. "Now please excuse me because I must go and supervise lunch."

"Lee (which is how Liberace is known to his friends), what is this idea you want to discuss with us?" asks Elvis.

It's a TV Special, to be shot in Las Vegas, featuring its two greatest entertainers – Elvis and himself. "This is so big that nobody ever thought it was possible to do before. We're the dream team and if we make it happen the TV people, sponsors and advertisers will lap it up," he goes on. "I can see it becoming a weekly show with a prime-time spot on Saturday nights. I mean, how can it fail?"

They can boost their fees by insisting on being paid as the producers as well as the stars. "Guests will want to pay us to appear on our show," he adds, beginning to sound remarkably like Colonel Parker in his approach to making money.

He has a great name for it – the Lee-Vis show with its play on their two names. He believes it is catchy enough for Levi Jeans to want to pay a fortune to be the sole sponsor.

The Colonel takes an instant dislike to the idea since it places Liberace's name before Elvis's. There is no way that's going to happen. As if it were a game of poker, he raises the stakes, proposing that it should be called the Elvis-Lee Yours TV Special.

Liberace smiles and takes a sip of his cocktail, knowing what is going on, but thinking that the best course is to get agreement to the idea of the show first and then worry about the name later.

"Let's take a break from talking about the TV Special for the time being," suggests Lee. "I'd like to show you something really cute. It's a great idea and I think I'm going to run with it, but first I'd like to hear what you guys think of it."

He waves a hand at Brother George who nods his head and walks away, returning with a black leather briefcase that looks very like the one Colonel Parker had. A cold shiver runs down his back and his mouth goes dry. He rubs his many layers of chins, hoping his suspicions are unfounded.

From the briefcase Liberace holds up an 18-inch-high doll that looks vaguely like him. "Isn't it just the cutest thing?" he coos.

The figure, which has grey bouffant hair and a fixed smile with big white teeth, is dressed in a white shiny suit and black bow tie.

"Listen to this," he continues. He lifts up the full-length cloak that looks as if it has made from rabbit fur to reveal a ring pull. He gives it a tug and, whilst it sounds thin and tinny, the doll is recognisably playing the opening to Beethoven's Fifth Symphony.

The Colonel looks at Elvis and Bubba in such a way that tells them to say nothing.

Treachery, he thinks. There must be a mole at Graceland who has leaked his secret plan to Liberace. When they get back there needs to be an investigation – something on the lines of the Spanish Inquisition should do the trick – to reveal the identity of the traitor.

Colonel Parker inquires, as casually as he can, what gave Liberace the idea to produce such a doll.

"It wasn't me. I was approached by this Chinese businessman called Ho Mee Cheep who said he could make them for about seventy-five cents each," he responds. "He says we would then sell them at twenty dollars each, with him taking fifteen dollars to cover his costs of production and distribution. Hey presto! I get the other five dollars for doing nothing!" He beams happily.

'The rat!' curses the Colonel to himself. It is the same guy who promoted the idea of the Elvis dolls to him. Now he is marketing it to somebody else. And if that wasn't serious enough, there is one big difference. The Elvis doll is due to retail at $25, with $5 going to Elvis, the same as Liberace. But Mr Ho Mee Cheep will be raking in $20 per doll on the deal. The only good thing to come out of this shocking revelation is that there isn't a viper in the nest at Graceland.

Colonel Parker has been suckered, and that makes him very dangerous. He will certainly attempt to renegotiate the contract at some considerable pain to the Chinese businessman, but first they need to eliminate the competition and dissuade Liberace from taking up the idea.

There is much frowning, sorrowful shaking of heads and sharp intakes of breath from the Colonel, Elvis and Bubba as they support each other in presenting a catalogue of reasons why the doll is such a bad idea: It is nothing like him; it looks and sounds cheap, whereas Liberace is known for his lavish outfits and accessories; and his fan base – predominantly middle-aged ladies – will be horrified by such tat being offered for sale.

Knowing what might happen further down the line with the proposed Elvis doll, the Colonel suggests that perhaps such an idea would be more appropriate for, say, a rock and roll singer and leaves it at that.

What kills it stone dead is when Elvis asks what his mother Frances thinks of it. As soon as she sees it, she pulls a face and declares: "Ugh! What on earth is that thing, Lee? Get rid of it at once!"

He looks crestfallen but puts it back in the briefcase. Colonel Parker, however, has a song in his heart as he, Elvis and Bubba set off to meet producer Hal Wallis for discussions about a possible new Elvis picture.

Charlie is sitting next to Elvis in a chair that belongs to the head electrician, but he has changed the word on the back from 'Gaffer' to 'Gofer'. He hands Elvis a cup of water, just as he does when they are on stage singing, and says he has a good feeling about the proposed movie but won't mention the 'O' word. Elvis looks at him quizzically; he leans closer and whispers "Oscar" in his ear.

The only possible relief for Elvis is the hope that his co-star will be Ann-Margret or Tuesday Weld, but he thinks that they are bringing in an English actress. He strokes his chin and works his way through the possibilities that include Elizabeth Taylor and Julie Christie. Charlie says that he has heard a rumour it might be somebody called Hattie Jacques.

Colonel Parker is playing cards with Hal Wallis when he's told that his assistant is on the phone for him from Graceland.

"Yes, Bubba," he snaps. "What is it? This is not a good time to call me. I'm talking about trying to shoot a new movie while playing gin rummy with Hal Wallis, so you can imagine how incredibly busy I am. And I'm not losing – I'm actually breaking even!!"

"That's wonderful news, sir. I've had a phone call from Mr Ho Mee Cheep saying that the consignment of Elvis dolls has left on a container ship, and he has provided an extra five thousand at no extra cost as per your new agreement." Bubba adds: "He said some things in Chinese which I didn't understand but I'm guessing he's not very happy."

"Probably not, but I am."

The news reports are calling it an environmental catastrophe. A sudden storm in the Pacific Ocean dislodges a container from a ship. As it falls into the sea it bursts open, releasing tens of thousands of Elvis dolls which then coalesce into one huge slick that is carried by the current towards Hawaii and its famous Waikiki Beach. Apparently, it is so big that, like the Great Wall of China, it can be seen from space.

Bubba is surprised how calmly the Colonel is taking the news. "Sir, you must be devastated; you must have lost a fortune when that container went overboard."

"Not at all," he replies, calmly rolling a cigar between his thumb and fingers as if he were assessing some expensive import from Havana rather than a special offer from Walmart.

"Always remember what the Colonel teaches you. It's strictly Cash on Delivery. In C.O.D. We Trust. No Show, No Dough. It hasn't cost us a dime."

Eerily, from different parts of the slick, thousands of voices of Elvis can be heard, siren-like, singing a tinny-sounding version of *C C Rider* as they ride the crest of the waves.

At first, fish such as sharks, dolphins, and whales, are intrigued by this strange, high-pitched sound, but having got nearer, they take fright and swim off in the opposite direction. It will be years before many species of fish return to the waters around Hawaii.

The Governor goes on TV to report: "I am sorry to say this about the King of Rock and Roll, but this advancing tsunami of Elvis dolls is a major threat to the environment and the tourist industry of Hawaii, the like of which has not been seen since Pearl Harbor."

As the strong winds relentlessly drive the huge slick of Elvis dolls towards Waikiki Beach the Governor says he has no alternative but to act quickly and decisively and to call in the Air Force to bomb them and stave off a very unnatural disaster.

Before he can do so he gets an urgent phone call from Colonel Parker who tells him: "Governor, how would you like to clean up Waikiki Beach for free, boost tourism and make a lot of money at the same time. But first you've got to call off this bombing mission. You don't have to declare war on Elvis."

"Colonel, you have my full attention."

In essence, the scheme proposed by Colonel Parker is a pick-your-own operation, but instead of fruit, customers will harvest Elvis dolls. First, the Governor must seal off the beach, citing health and safety reasons. This means that only visitors – or 'collectors', as he prefers to call them – who have bought special Elvis nets and buckets will be allowed on to the beach to rescue up to five Elvises of their choice, for which they will then pay a modest $5 each. He will also organise gold standard charter flights for people who will be allowed to salvage an unlimited number of Elvis dolls providing, of course, they pay $5 for each one.

"Don't you think that five dollars might be a bit excessive for something that has been washed up after floating in the sea for couple of weeks?" asks the Governor.

"I'm told by the manufacturer," he replies, "that these dolls are highly engineered, using technology first pioneered by NASA."

The Governor is about to ask if they sent an Elvis doll into space but thinks better of it. However, he does ask if it would be a good idea to promote the event as a kind of fiesta or Mardi Gras.

"I agree," replies Colonel Parker. "We should call it the 'Elvisly Yours Fishing Festival'. It has a certain catchiness to it." (*'Catchiness'* he says to himself. *I just made a joke!*) And of course, there remains the issue of agreeing a commission for my assistance."

There is a long pause, and the Colonel detects a loud sigh before the Governor continues: "I'll have to think about that. What might help me decide is if Elvis... and, er... yourself, of course, were to come to Hawaii for the festival and put on a show. That would really boost the number of visitors, I mean 'collectors'."

There is silence from the other end of the phone.

"I'll add another ten per cent to your commission," suggests the Governor.

"Make it twenty-five per cent and get the garlands ready. We'll be there."

"It's a deal."

There is a huge audience of 'collectors' watching the show on a stage set up on Waikiki Beach. Elvis and the TCB band have agreed to donate their fees to an Hawaiian environmental charity. However, by some administrative oversight, which he has promised to investigate, Colonel Parker's commission is not included in the donation.

The show opens with the Colonel's troupe of dancing chickens performing a brand-new routine to *Hawaiian Wedding Song*. The only other act is Elvis who appears on stage in a bright red Hawaiian shirt, a garland of flowers around his neck and a deep tan applied by Larry Geller, his personal hairdresser.

At one point Elvis halts the show and asks the audience to be as quiet as possible. "I want a big shush, please. Listen very carefully. Can you hear it?"

They can just make out the distant sound of the dolls, even after all this time in the water, still mechanically singing *C C Rider*. It produces a huge cheer from the audience.

After closing his hour-long set with *Can't Help Falling in Love* he makes his way to the gate as the announcer declares: "Ladies and Gentlemen, Elvis has left the building."

Elvis stands at the head of a vast throng, holding a net and bucket high above his head like a regimental standard, while the Governor makes a short speech, fires a starting pistol, and opens the gate.

Elvis sets off across the sand at a steady jog but is quickly left behind; he's not worried, knowing that his participation is purely ceremonial, but he is surprised by how quickly he is being overtaken. He is unaware that some of the 'collectors' have been in training to be ready for the sprint to the surf, while others have hired Olympic athletes to make sure they are first to scoop up the dolls that are in the best condition; others have enlisted American football stars who can knock over anybody in their way in the dash to the sea.

By the time Elvis gets there a frenzy has developed when it becomes apparent that there are significantly less of the G.I. Blues dolls than the others, and 'collectors' are racing up and down the beach or wading out to sea in search of one of them. Scuffles break out when someone spots one floating in the surf. Elvis realises he must act before things get ugly.

There are shouts of "Listen up everybody. It's the King. He wants to speak" from among the crowd as Elvis tries to restore order.

He says that he can't explain why there are so many less of the G.I. Blues dolls than the others – maybe they are less buoyant. However, he knows it is a typical ploy used by his manager to drive up interest and sales. Therefore, it is up to him to sort it out.

"I know this may take a little time and I want you all to be patient. Here's what to do: write to Colonel Parker, my manager, at Graceland; he will arrange for more of these dolls to be produced and everybody who writes to him will get one."

How much will they cost, the crowd wants to know.

"Five dollars, the same as today," he assures them.

There are cheers and applause for the King, and everybody is happy with Elvis's compromise. Apart from Colonel Parker, whose office is soon deluged with a tsunami of letters from the collectors of Elvis dolls.

US Mail sacks are heaped in a corner of his office, taunting him to do something to make them go away. He waves his cigar miserably in their direction. "Five dollars! Jeez, Bubba, I'll struggle to make a dime on every sale."

"Who's going to make them, sir? I don't think it will be Mr Ho Mee Cheep. Not after what has happened and him saying he'd been screwed."

"Hmm," says the Colonel, as he fans away the circling cloud of cigar smoke with his straw trilby.

"Here's the thing, Bubba," he says. "I wonder if he actually made any of those Liberace dolls. If he did, we might be in business. All we'd need to do is dye the hair black and we've got Elvis!"

There's a sharp intake of breath from Bubba, followed by a sad shake of the head. "I'm not so sure about that, sir, and besides, Elvis's act doesn't include Beethoven's Fifth Symphony which the doll plays."

"Maybe we can get him to change his act."

THE RETIREMENT HOME FOR ELVIS TRIBUTE ARTISTS

Colonel Parker is concerned. It's most unlike him, but Elvis arrived in his office at Graceland in a fickle mood, and he'll need to make inquiries later to find out what's behind it. He laughed – yes, laughed! – at his idea for an 'Aloha from Alaska' TV Christmas Special. It could become a regular feature in the TV schedules, he explained. But that provoked a fit of giggles. "Why don't we have one called 'Howdy from Texas' or 'Y'all have a nice day from Georgia'," sniggered Elvis.

Now he insists on hearing an appeal from the If I Can Dream retirement home for Elvis tribute artists, despite his manager's protests that it should go in the wastepaper bin along with all the other begging letters that were delivered that day.

Bubba, the Colonel's assistant, reads out the letter: "We are a charity that is already looking after a hundred retired Elvis tribute artists, but there are more who have fallen on hard times. We don't want to turn them away, to be left on the showbusiness scrapheap after they have provided so much entertainment and pleasure. We are asking if Elvis, the King, and our idol, will help this worthy cause."

The letter, adds Bubba, is signed by a Colonel Tim Packer.

Colonel Parker bangs his fist on his desk at this final insult – a parody of his name.

"How dare they!" he bellows. "They take money with their tenth-rate imitations of Elvis, when they have zero talent themselves, and they never pay a single cent to the man they are ripping off. They steal his identity, his fame, his act, and his songs.

"And now, can you believe it, somebody who is making fun of my good name, a name that's a byword in the industry for integrity, has the colossal cheek to come begging for even more money! It's outrageous!"

His indignation has caused his face to go bright red and beads of sweat run down in rivulets, like the Nile Delta, through the stubble on his layers of chins. He removes his straw trilby to fan himself and dab his face with a dingy-looking handkerchief.

"Just hold on there a minute, Colonel, sir," says Elvis. "There's another way of looking at this."

The fact that Elvis may be about to express an opinion, and one that contradicts his own, comes as another shock to Colonel Parker, whose day is plummeting from bad to worse. What was to be his latest triumph – his plans for 'Aloha from Alaska' – is being supplanted by a conversation about has-been Elvis impersonators.

"The way I see it is all these tribute acts have created an ever-expanding World of Elvis. There are thousands of wannabe Elvises performing every day. That means I am constantly kept at the forefront of my fans' minds. Of course, they know it's not me they're watching. But I believe it makes my fans want to see me, the real Elvis, to see my shows, watch my movies and let's not forget this, Colonel, buy your merchandise."

He adds, "I don't think we should be too hasty in ignoring this appeal."

Colonel Parker sits silently puffing on his special offer Walmart cigar. He may not want to admit it, since he styles himself as always being the one who takes care of business, but Elvis has made a very good point. He needs a comeback.

"But the fact remains we don't know who these people are," he declares. "It could be one great big con. Does this If I Can Dream retirement home actually exist?"

"Yes, it does," responds Bubba. "It's on the outskirts of Las Vegas."

"Las Vegas! They've probably gambled their money away on The Strip!" roars the Colonel. "First, we must find out more about this so-called charity," he continues. "For all we know they could be living the life of Riley, fine dining and lounging around all day, waiting for their next big cash handout from some unsuspecting benefactor like Elvis. The next thing you know they'll be opening a new retirement home in The Hamptons."

Elvis nods his head, reluctantly agreeing with his manager's advice.

"I'm not saying we won't help in some way or other, but let's get some facts about them. Give me time to think about how we can do it," concludes the Colonel.

Twenty-four hours later he is still trying to figure out a way. What he needs to do is to talk to a resident who is willing to spill the beans or send in a spy pretending to be an Elvis impersonator who's down on his luck. However, it would need to be somebody convincing...

There's a tap-tap-tap on the door of his office. He knows who it is but decides to torment him by ignoring it. Annoying Charlie Hodge is one of life's small pleasures for Elvis's manager.

The knocking becomes louder and longer, and he responds by cupping a hand to his ear and asking if anyone else can hear a noise. "I think it might be woodworm eating into the door," he sniggers. "I must have a word with the pest control people."

Bubba intervenes. "I think it's Charlie Hodge, sir. He said he'd like to see you and Elvis."

Colonel Parker takes a few puffs of a particularly foul-smelling cigar and makes a play of leafing through the pages of his diary. Finally, he nods to his assistant to let him in.

"Ah, I see it isn't woodworm after all. Come in Charlie and pull up a chair. There's not much happening here that we can't interrupt – just a few minor details that Elvis and I are trying to organise for his next tour; you know the sort of thing: booking stadiums, ticket sales, publicity, merchandising, travel arrangements, hotel accommodation. But never mind, I'll put all that on hold. What can we do for you? Not run out of furniture polish, have you, or those very expensive monogrammed dusters you like to use?"

One of Charlie's tasks, when he is not performing with Elvis, is to look after the housework at Graceland. His response to the sarcasm is a grimace.

"There's a suggestion that I'd like to put to Elvis and you, to see what you think," he states. "My fans are asking if I can do a solo spot during Elvis's shows, perhaps during the interval."

Colonel Parker looks utterly perplexed as if he has been speaking in Chinese. He asks Elvis if he knows anything about this; he shakes his head and studies his boots, fearing that his oldest friend, booster-in-chief and gofer may be in for a very uncomfortable few minutes of interrogation.

"What sort of thing do you have in mind? Juggling, conjuring tricks, ventriloquism? I know of lot of carny people who can do that sort of thing and who'd do it for nothing as a favour to me."

"The idea is that I should sing a few songs."

The Colonel laughs uproariously, stopping eventually to wipe his eyes and blow his nose on a faded souvenir 'Loving You' handkerchief.

"Amuse us, Charlie: what sort of songs?" he asks.

"Obviously, I wouldn't do any of Elvis's material."

"Thank goodness for that! It will be a relief to Elvis, all his fans and me!"

"I was thinking I could perform some of the old country and gospel songs I did when I was with the Scratchy Bottom Boys."

"And you say that the idea for this musical interlude has come from your fans."

"Yes, the members of the Charlie Hodge International Fan Club."

Colonel Parker scrutinises the ceiling rendered dark yellow by years of cigar smoke while he searches, like Perry Mason, for the killer question.

He comes up with: "How many fan club members are we talking about?"

"As we speak, six nurses in Decatur," whispers Charlie.

There are times when the Colonel has excellent hearing. Where invoices are concerned, for example, he is stone deaf. This is one of those occasions when he hears every word.

"How do you think this foolishness will go down with all the members of Elvis's fan clubs around the world? Remind us, what sort of numbers of are we talking about, Bubba?"

"The last time we did a count it was twenty million, sir. But the numbers keep rising exponentially."

Colonel Parker bursts out laughing again and goes into his routine of wiping his eyes and blowing his nose. "That's a lot more than six. This is so funny. Wait till I tell Jack Benny. He'll want to use this – word for word, I swear – in his next show. But he'll need to have medical assistance on standby because people in the audience will die laughing."

He looks meaningfully at Elvis before going on: "I know he will agree with me, but Elvis shows feature only Elvis – no guest appearances, no breakout spots for members of the band. That's the rule, that's how it's always been and always will be. It's fixed in stone, and we won't change it for you and your six fans."

Charlie is crestfallen and gets up to leave the office.

"Hold on there a moment, Charlie," calls out the Colonel. A light bulb has switched on in his head and he realises he has found the answer to his problem: the perfect patsy.

"An opportunity has just come up for you to perform a great service to Elvis and me. Are you interested? Good. Come back tomorrow and we'll explain, and I promise it's a starring role."

The meeting resumes next day with Colonel Parker telling Charlie about the request they've received for financial help from a home that looks after retired Elvis tribute singers.

He puts on his rarely seen sincere face and says, "Elvis is anxious to do the right thing, but before we do anything we want to investigate to see if it is genuine or a con.

"The best way to find out the truth is to send in somebody undercover as an Elvis impersonator who's looking to live there so he can 'case the joint'. It needs to be somebody completely convincing, who knows Elvis and his songs because you can't fool them – they'd soon spot a phoney. That's why we've picked you."

First, he explains, they need to create an identity for him in his role as an Elvis tribute artist. He claps his hands, a door opens and Bernard Lansky, the man who designs all Elvis's stage outfits, walks in pushing a mannequin on wheels.

"We give you... Paddy Elvis!" declares Colonel Parker.

Charlie is aghast. "No! Never!"

The mannequin is wearing a bright green jumpsuit with a large shamrock picked out in green and white crystals on the chest; the trousers are cut off just below the knee to reveal long orange socks; there's a tall green hat; and the outfit is finished off with a bushy ginger beard.

"I'm not Irish! Why do you want me to be a leprechaun?"

"Begorrah!" laughs the Colonel, who cannot resist saying it. "You're small. We thought it would be a good fit."

"I'll be your secret undercover agent, but please, not as Paddy Elvis." He turns to Elvis, holding his hands together in a gesture of prayer. Being Elvis's oldest friend and trusted gofer carries a lot of weight, and Charlie wins a reprieve.

He sets off for the If I Can Dream retirement home in a Vegas stage jumpsuit, with some last-minute adaptations by Bernard Lansky, as well as some flourishes from Larry Geller, Elvis's personal hair stylist. He is now known as Tiny Elvis.

Charlie is taken to the office of Colonel Tim Packer, who sent the appeal letter to Elvis. He is slim, clean-shaven, aged about 40, and polite. The only thing he has in common with Colonel Tom Parker is the bright orange Hawaiian shirt he is wearing.

"So, you're Tiny Elvis," he says, shaking Charlie's hand. "I understand you're here on a visit to find out more about our home with a view to possibly coming to live here among our community of retired Elvis tribute artists. By the way, my name is Richard. I suppose you could call me a Colonel Parker tribute act, which works well in the sort of establishment we run here."

He pretends to puff on a cigar, but starts to laugh and quickly puts it down, saying that it's plastic and a prop.

He explains that the retirement home is a former holiday camp where college kids used to go during their summer vacations. There is a central complex of buildings that includes offices, residents' lounge, kitchen and dining room, gymnasium, sick bay, bar, and a hall with a stage; it is circled by blocks of apartments where the residents live.

"We chose it because the guys said they wanted to be close to where the action is," he continues. "That means Las Vegas which was a big part of their lives. Some of the younger ones still get the occasional bits of work performing in the bars and restaurants on The Strip, or sometimes at weddings and funerals.

"We were able to set up the retirement home because the guys all used a chunk of their savings to buy shares. We try to keep going with what they earn from their bookings, donations from fans and the occasional bequest. But it is never enough."

He invites Charlie to come and meet some of the residents. "I'm sure you'll find out a lot more of what you want to know by talking to them."

Charlie is momentarily stopped in his tracks as the door opens to the lounge and he finds himself in a time warp. Like the Jungle Room at Graceland, it is similarly furnished with a green, faux fur carpet, animal prints, African masks, and plants.

He has barely recovered from that shock when he is introduced to someone dressed in a black jumpsuit with a design on the chest of a tombstone bearing the letters R.I.P. To his horror he recognises him as Scary Elvis, who attended the school for wannabe Elvis tribute acts at Graceland (see Professor Elvis in Elvis & A Royal Visit). *Please don't let him remember who I am,* he thinks to himself as he sits next to him.

"Hi, I'm Tiny Elvis," he says.

Scary Elvis smiles, revealing a set of vampire fangs. "Pleased to meet you. You can probably guess what sort of act I did. What did you do?"

"Mainly children's parties and that sort of thing, but the work is drying up. Maybe I'm getting too old to be entertaining kids. When did you retire?"

"I'm still in rehab and I've not been able to work for nearly a year. They used to carry me on stage in a coffin. I'd let out a blood-curdling scream, slowly lift the coffin lid and start singing. I was performing *Suspicious Minds* and was down on one knee and twirling my arm round and round, like Elvis does, when everything suddenly locked. I couldn't move. I went on stage in a coffin and left on a stretcher. When we got to ER, I heard one of the doctors shout, 'It's another Elvis.' He told me: 'Don't worry, sir, we've done this sort of thing many times before.'"

Charlie looks around the room and counts about 60 Vegas Elvises in their white jumpsuits, jet black wigs and airline pilot glasses. In contrast, there are only two Comeback Special Elvises, and one G.I. Elvis. What does it say about Elvis's career as the King of Rock and Roll?

What about the Sun years, and the great movies like *Jailhouse Rock* and *King Creole*?

He nods to Scary Elvis and, as he gets up to go and talk to another resident, a man carrying a suitcase walks in and sits down at a table. As one, all the Elvises scramble to their feet and rush to line up. There is some jostling to get to the head of the queue.

"What's going on?" he asks.

"It's Doctor Mick," replies an Elvis barging past him. "It's his surgery."

"Why aren't you joining the queue?" says another. "Is there something wrong with you?" Oh, the irony, thinks Charlie. For form's sake, he decides to make his way to the end of the line.

From what he can make out, the consultations consist of Dr Mick making notes of their complaints; prescribing various pills, ointments, and syrups; and making appointments to treat them in the sick bay. They should all thank their lucky stars, he thinks, because he hasn't heard any mention of enemas, the treatment favoured by Dr Nick, Elvis's personal physician, for all complaints.

When it's finally his turn Dr Mick remarks, "You're new, aren't you?" He makes a note that he is a visitor, and his name is Tiny Elvis. "What's the problem? How long are you staying here?" He wears a gold medallion and gold bracelets like Dr Nick.

Charlie tells him, "Overnight, and it's just a bit of a headache."

He walks away with a box of aspirin.

After dinner he joins the rest of the residents in the hall for that evening's entertainment, which always follows the same pattern: one of the Elvises performs his act, followed by an Elvis movie.

Tonight, it is the turn of Johnny Reb Elvis, whose jumpsuit resembles the uniform of a Confederate soldier. He finishes his act by singing *American Trilogy* while vigorously waving a Confederate flag. Charlie surmises that he probably never got much work north of the Mason Dixon Line.

Colonel Packer walks out to the front of the audience. "Oh, what a treat we have for you with our movie tonight," he declares. "Yes, it's back by popular request. I give you... *Kissin' Cousins*."

The announcement unleashes a barrage of whoops and hollers, the stamping of feet and a solitary rebel yell.

"They really seem to like this film," Charlie comments to a neighbour. He'd never dare admit it, but he'd put it near the bottom of the King's 31 movies.

"You bet," he answers. "It's double Elvis. We get two for the price of one because he plays two look-alike cousins."

Next morning Charlie goes to the office of Colonel Tim Packer to tell him that he is leaving. He comes from behind his desk to shake his hand. "I hope you've enjoyed your stay with us, Charlie," he says.

He blushes and stammers, "You know who I am?"

"Of course, we do. We recognised you right away, even with the dyed blond hair and the moustache. You're always there at Elvis's side at every show he does. We guessed why you came to visit us, because of my letter. We decided to let you continue with your pretence. We hope you liked what you saw, and you'll tell Elvis about the work we do here because there are more Elvis tribute acts that desperately need our help."

Charlie blushes a deeper red. "I'm sorry, Colonel Packer... I mean, Richard... about the subterfuge. Elvis is a very generous person and helps many good causes. But there are others who try to take advantage of his kindness. We just wanted to be sure about the If I Can Dream retirement home."

"Yes, I understand."

"Pardon me for asking this, but I'm curious to know, and Elvis will be, too: Why is the retirement home a sort of copy of Graceland, with things like you as Colonel Tim Packer, a Dr Mick and a Jungle Room?"

He replies: "Elvis is the embodiment of the American Dream, the man with a God-given talent who came from nowhere to become the King of Rock and Roll and the greatest entertainer in the world. He's their idol, the person they'd all aspire to be. Through their tribute acts they become Elvis themselves. And by making the retirement home here where they live into a little bit like Graceland, it makes them feel part of his family, and that brings them closer to him."

Charlie is impressed by what he has seen in the short time he's been there. While he cannot speak for Elvis, he believes it is a cause worthy of his support. And that is what he will recommend.

They say their goodbyes and as he steps outside the office, he hears an announcement on the PA system: "Charlie Hodge is leaving the building." It is a nice gesture that makes him feel good and to walk a little bit taller. Some of the residents are lined up at the entrance to pat him on the back and wish him well. "Give our regards to Elvis," they call after him.

Elvis, Charlie, and Bubba glance at each other and shake their heads as Colonel Parker goes into his pantomime routine, flinching as if he has been skewered by a sword. His hand reaches for his heart, except that where it should be, there's a wallet; his eyes roll, and he lets out a deep groan.

It's his reaction to Elvis telling him that he'd like to make a substantial cash donation to the If I Can Dream retirement home. Charlie says that his visit has convinced him that it is a worthwhile cause, and that's his recommendation to Elvis.

The Colonel glares at him. "Bubba, make a note that Charlie Hodge would like his name to be at the top of the list of donors."

Charlie gulps. He doesn't think he is kidding.

He continues, "Elvis, let me point out the obvious, that giving away money is bad for business. Where will it end? I mean, what possible benefit is there in setting yourself up as a soft touch?"

Ticking off the points on his fingers, Elvis answers: "Let me see, off the top of my head, there's doing the right thing; helping people in need; generating goodwill; and setting an example to other people. And do you know what? You can add that it makes me feel good."

Colonel Parker shakes his head in bewilderment. He also notes the touch of belligerence in his response. He sags in his chair, like a balloon losing air and slowly shrivelling up.

"There's some good news, sir, that might cheer you up," says Bubba. "Bear in mind that you get tax relief on the money you give to charity." He winks at Elvis and Charlie.

The Colonel begins to reinflate as if he has been connected to a pump. He's back to his old self in a matter of seconds – plumped up, alert and concentrating. He lights a new cigar which he jabs in the direction of his assistant.

"Bubba, did my ears deceive me? But did you just say the magic words 'tax relief'?"

"Yes, sir, the bigger the donation, the more tax relief you get."

"Boys, I believe you have just made an excellent business case why we should support such a worthwhile cause."

He gazes up at the dark yellow, nicotine-stained ceiling, searching for inspiration. Waving his cigar airily, he tells them: "I see a benefit show being staged at the International Hotel in Las Vegas. Every seat is sold. Wait – there's more. With such a heart-warming story as this, I can also see it being shown in a two-part series on prime-time TV: first, the documentary, and then the show. Leave it to me."

As Elvis gets up to go Colonel Parker adds: "Of course, there is an unfortunate consequence. I'll have to put my plans for 'Aloha from Alaska' on ice for the time being if I'm to give this project my full attention."

"Sorry to hear that, sir," replies Elvis, shaking his head. "Such a sacrifice."

As soon as he steps outside the office, he bursts out laughing and punches the air in triumph.

At the end of the show, a spotlight picks out Priscilla as she emerges from the wings. Her short, metallic silver dress reflects the light like a brilliant, dazzling comet crossing the sky as she makes her way towards the centre of the stage. Her designer, Edith Head, assured her that the outfit's impact would draw the TV cameras to her like moths to a flame. She carries a big cardboard cheque from the Bank of Jefferson Davis, made out to the If I Can Dream retirement home, in the sum of $500,000. She and Elvis present it to Richard, aka Colonel Tim Packer, who receives it on behalf of the charity.

In organising the benefit show, Colonel Parker took to heart the advice about charitable donations being tax deductible. He's decided that when the time comes for him to submit his tax returns – and that will only happen after receiving a final warning in large red capital letters from the IRS – he will make a small error and claim that the amount given to the retirement home charity was $5 million, not $500,000. One nought too many – an easy mistake to make when there are so many noughts! Of course, he will apologise – should it ever come to light.

There is also an oversight regarding the revenue from all the merchandise sold at the show. In the very small print on page 34 of the contract, it states that all such income is not part of the monies to be donated to the retirement home.

"*Silly me,*" he chuckles to himself, "*to forget something like that. I should know better.*"

Holding hands, Elvis and Priscilla walk to the front of the stage and beckon to the 100 tribute artists, sitting together in the centre of the front stalls, to invite them to join them. The response is a burst of clapping, cheers, and a few wheezy whistles. They line up to take turns climbing the stairs at the side of the stage; however, some of the more elderly and infirm are so slow that Colonel Parker wishes he'd hired a stairlift.

The medical attendants, who look on anxiously in case somebody keels over, decide to carry Wheelie Elvis up the stairs before reuniting him with his wheelchair.

Finally, it is the turn of Chubby Elvis. It's a struggle, even with two people pulling from the top and three more pushing from below, to try and get him up the stairs and on to the stage. The audience joins in, encouraging them with shouts of "Heave-ho!"

The If I Can Dream retirement home will always be grateful for the $500,000 that Elvis has helped to raise, and the priceless publicity he generated for the charity. As a result, another 25 retired tribute acts are accommodated at the home.

But they agree that his greatest gift was to summon them all to share the stage with him. Before they retired, they'd spent years presenting their version of Elvis, in their home-made outfits, usually in small venues before small audiences. Now they've appeared on network TV at the International Hotel in Las Vegas – a choir of 100 Elvis tribute artists clustered around the King himself, who led them in singing his traditional show-closer *Can't Help Falling in Love*.

In those few minutes he made all their dreams come true.

TOO MUCH MONKEY BUSINESS

Charlie Hodge drives on to the car park of the small mission hall in downtown Memphis. The paint on the wooden boards of the building is dingy brown and peeling, it has a corrugated iron roof, and the noticeboard proclaims, 'Running on Empty? Fill Up Here on Sundays' and 'Keep Calm and Carry on Praying'. Surely this cannot be the right place for an animal training class; after all, he doesn't want to go to a revivalist meeting. But there is no mistake when he checks the address on the piece of paper given to him by Bubba, Colonel Parker's assistant.

He unclips Scatter, Elvis's pet chimpanzee, from his seat in the back of the Lincoln Continental and takes his hand to walk him into the mission hall. For once, he is subdued but that's probably because he's away from Graceland where he feels at home and able to run riot, and because was seen by Dr Nick, Elvis's personal physician, before they left.

On entering the room they find 15 people sitting on chairs in a circle, facing each other, like old folks do in retirement homes; with them are their pets: dogs, mainly puppies, yapping at each other and eager to be let off their leashes; three cats that stare mournfully from their cages; a snake coiled around a guy's neck; and a tortoise on the floor chewing a piece of lettuce.

Charlie can sense that Scatter is feeling tense; possibly he's spooked by the strange surroundings and all the other animals. He says a silent prayer and hopes for the best that things will go quietly.

The room smells fusty and the draught from a single open window stirs the dust motes like a slowly moving murmuration of starlings. At the back there is a small stage with the curtains drawn, and dangling from the rafters are things Charlie hasn't seen for years – spirals of sticky fly papers, heavily encrusted with dead flies. They've probably been there since the Civil War.

The guy in charge, who introduces himself as Jerry Bilt, has a grey beard of the style once favoured by President Lincoln and very bushy eyebrows like garden hedges; he is dressed in a grey cardigan, brown corduroy trousers, battered leather sandals and no socks.

He welcomes Charlie to the Happy Ever After animal training class, while looking quizzically at Scatter, dressed in a white jumpsuit with the slogan 'Champ Chimp' emblazoned in rhinestones on the chest.

"Well, I do declare, I think he's our first monkey! Please introduce yourselves to the rest of the class."

"The chimpanzee's name is Scatter, but he's no ordinary chimp," he answers proudly. "In fact, he's Elvis's chimp."

There's an involuntary gasp, followed by an awed hush around the room. "Elvis!" "The King!" they say excitedly to each other and inch their chairs forward into a tighter circle so as not to miss a word.

Charlie introduces himself as Elvis's personal assistant (he's thought about this on the drive there and feels it has the right sort of gravitas, much better than the term gofer). He explains that Scatter has been spoiled, not by Elvis, he adds hastily and without blushing. However, he has become badly behaved and needs to learn some discipline – quickly.

Charlie understands that these training classes may be the make or break for the chimpanzee who is on borrowed time. Elvis is very fond of him and finds his antics hilarious, and that's Scatter's ace in the hole. But everybody else in Graceland is involved in various plots to bring about his downfall.

Charlie was present a couple of days ago when Scatter suddenly appeared in the kitchen. Minnie Mae, Elvis's grandmother, waved a long filleting knife in his direction and gave him the evil eye. Scatter whimpered and scuttled away.

"Ah swear ah'm a-gonna fricassee that hairy wrecking ball afore the next full moon," she muttered to herself.

As if on cue, Scatter bares his teeth at the other animals in the hall and starts to scream and hop up and down. Breaking free from Charlie's grip, he runs towards the stage, picking up a dog bowl on the way which he waves above his head as if it were a weapon.

The result is a deafening pandemonium. All the dogs are barking, leaping up and straining against their leashes to break free and chase after him, while their owners fight to restrain them, shouting things like "Down boy" and "Bruce, you bad boy". Chairs are sent flying in the struggle, the cats hiss and spit, arch their backs and retreat deeper into their cages, and the tortoise ducks into its shell. Apparently, it will be months before it emerges again.

Still screaming, Scatter scampers up one of the curtains, pulling it down in the process; he pauses to throw the bowl to the floor, and then swings among the rafters, tearing down the spirals of fly papers as he goes, and hurling them to the floor. Some of the dogs break free and circle below Scatter like a pack of wolves, barking and howling. Pets that normally play with cuddly toys have developed a blood lust.

Jerry Bild holds his head in his hands and repeats, "No, no, no." Weeks of training have been wiped out and rendered useless within five minutes of Scatter's arrival.

Meanwhile, the chimpanzee ignores the chaos below, and concentrates on tasting some of the dead flies which he removes from one of the spirals of sticky fly paper.

"Get some bananas quick and get him down," Jerry yells at Charlie.

"Bananas – no, he wouldn't get out of bed for bananas," he responds. Charlie thinks hard, concentration creasing his forehead. As if inspired, he announces: "Hershey bars, he's partial to Hershey bars. That might do it."

One of the dog owners remembers that he has a packet of chocolate drop treats. Once the dogs are back on their leashes, Charlie tosses up a couple of chocolate drops to Scatter to get him interested. Yes, he prefers them to dead flies, so Charlie runs a trail along the floor to the front door where he recaptures him.

All the other pet owners slump back in their chairs, shell-shocked, apart from the man who is crawling around on his hands and knees, trying to find where his snake is hiding.

"Sorry about that," says Charlie, taking a last look around before leaving. Scatter has turned the meeting hall into a war zone. "I know he can be a bit boisterous. See you again, same time next week." As a parting shot Scatter throws up, having eaten too much chocolate and too many dead flies.

They go back a week later but find the doors locked and the hall empty. The caretaker informs him that Mr Bilt's animal training class has cancelled all its bookings with immediate effect. He's aware they've moved to different premises, but he can't understand, despite being pressed, why Mr Bilt wouldn't tell him the new address.

Scatter seems disappointed; perhaps he'll miss the mayhem that he caused on their first visit. The problem remains that he needs training on how to be behave, and it must happen fast. Charlie takes him back to the car, recognising that there is a big question mark over the chimp's future at Graceland.

Most of the sections of the newspapers delivered each day to Graceland are ignored, apart from the funnies, which is taken by the guys to read in the Jungle Room. They're on tenterhooks, waiting to keep up with the daily adventures of Little Orphan Annie, Peanuts, Spiderman, Buck Ryan, and the rest. For the likes of Red and Sonny, the West cousins, who have graduated to reading the speech bubbles as well as looking at the illustrations, it is exhausting and can take the best part of a morning to read them all. Afterwards, they need a nap before lunch.

It's by chance that Bubba happens to glance at the front page of the Memphis Daily News, left neatly folded and unread on a table in the hall; he notices a small but intriguing news item that reports that the Museum of Modern Art in New York has paid $5,000 for a single painting by a chimpanzee. That's a lot of money for something that looks in the picture like a daub to Bubba's uncritical eye. Given that Graceland has its own chimpanzee, he mentions it to Colonel Parker when he goes into his office.

"For that kind of money, it must have been done by a famous chimp," declares the Colonel. "Was it Cheeta, Tarzan's monkey?"

"No, sir, it appears to have been painted by some ordinary, run-of-the-mill chimpanzee."

Bubba is startled: Colonel Parker is smiling, something that happens once in a blue moon. In fact, his assistant notes, it is almost a grin. He sits in his chair, with his hands resting on the huge protuberance of his stomach, looking as benign as Buddha.

"Five thousand dollars," he muses. "Imagine what the art galleries and Elvis's fans will pay for a painting, not by some no-account chimp, but by Elvis's chimp!"

"It will also be a useful way of keeping him busy and out of mischief," adds Bubba.

"That's an important bonus," agrees the Colonel. "It's about time that pest started earning his keep. I'll mention it at dinner in my usual diplomatic way. By the way, I think it's wise not to say anything about selling paintings for the time being. Let's not over-excite everybody. Remember the saying: 'Softly, softly, catchee monkey'. Ha ha ha."

Elvis thinks it has a civilising influence on Scatter if he eats with everybody else from time to time, and that he'll learn by example. Tonight is one of those occasions. Minnie Mae has provided a selection of fruit on his plate, fringed by several Hershey bars; on top is an avocado that she has peeled but left the stone inside, in the hope that the chimp will break several of his teeth when he bites into it.

Scatter is immediately attracted to it – because of its grenade-like shape. He lobs it at Colonel Parker sitting at the other end of the table, but he easily swerves out of the way. The avocado lands with a mushy plop against the wall and then commences its slow slide down to the floor.

Elvis roars with laughter, and he carries on laughing when the chimpanzee climbs on to the table and walks over to help himself to a handful of battered chitlins from Vernon's plate. Almost everybody is horrified and not sure what to do because Elvis thinks it's funny. The exception is Minnie Mae who picks up the soup ladle and cracks Scatter hard on the top of his head. The chimpanzee shouts out in pain, rubs his head, and runs out of the room.

"Oh dear, ah surely am real sorry," she says. "How clumsy of me. Ah wus jest a-tryin' ter serve him a helpin' o' chitlins."

Priscilla stares down at her plate of rocket and slices of cucumber, trying not to laugh. "Never mind, accidents will happen. But it looks like he's lost his appetite."

Scatter's appalling table manners have played into Colonel Parker's hands. Hal Wallis's scriptwriters could not have produced a better outcome.

He puts on a kindly, caring expression, one that he has been practising that afternoon, and comments that now might be the right time to mention his idea to improve Scatter's behaviour.

"What he needs is something to stimulate his mind, something that engages his enthusiasm and his energy and keeps him from getting into mischief." He pauses to heighten the dramatic effect before announcing: "What he needs is a hobby."

"You mean like stamp collecting?" asks Elvis's father, Vernon.

"Perhaps that's a bit fiddly for a chimp," replies the Colonel. "I was thinking more on the lines of painting. All those blank canvases to cover and all those bright colours to use."

He glances meaningfully at Bubba and then adds in a jovial Father Christmas sort of way, to underline what an amusing, throwaway remark it is: "Who knows, he might even produce a masterpiece."

"I like the sound of it," declares Elvis.

"It's not like you, Colonel. You haven't mentioned what the cost might be of this little venture," comments Priscilla.

Elvis waves his hand as if he is swatting away a fly. "It doesn't matter. I just want to see the little guy happy and having fun."

Priscilla continues to study her long, red-varnished nails while insisting, "That monkey won't be getting anywhere near a paint brush inside this house. Am I making myself very clear?"

Elvis gets the message.

A large shed is erected near the stables and generously stocked with easels, canvases, pots of paint and brushes. Vernon draws the short straw for the job of supervising Scatter and his painting activities. To make the assignment more appealing, a small bower with a sofa bed is erected where he can doze while the chimpanzee attempts to create a Mona Lisa while locked inside the shed.

Scatter seems to miss the point. Brushes are chewed and snapped in half, and a lot of paint is thrown on the walls and the floor, but so far none of it has landed on a canvas. Although he may be having fun destroying everything, which is exactly what his critics said would happen, Elvis was hoping that there'd be one or two paintings at least to prove them wrong.

Colonel Parker sits in his office, glumly contemplating the failure of his painting project: all that expense and nothing to show for it. "It looks like that chimp has made a monkey out of me," he comments ruefully to his assistant, Bubba. "After all I did for him. The ingratitude. We should be on Easy Street. How could it go so badly wrong?"

He thinks he'll cheer himself up by going through a pile of invoices and rejecting as many as possible.

"I wonder, sir, if you have heard of Picasso?"

The Colonel shakes his head. "No. Is he in carny?"

"No, sir."

"A circus performer, perhaps? With a name like that it sounds like he should be a clown. Lots of clowns have Italian names."

"Actually, sir, he's a painter. I've been doing some research, and his paintings sell for millions of dollars."

He sweeps the piles of invoices from his desk into a wastepaper basket with the back of his hand. "Bubba, you have my complete attention."

"It's an idea you might want to consider, sir. But if it is to succeed, you may have to find somebody else to manage the chimpanzee instead of Vernon."

"I'm listening…"

At the Colonel's suggestion, the mantle of being Scatter's muse passes to Aunt Delta, daughter of Minnie Mae, and the grumpiest person in Graceland. With her puffy, square-shaped face, small eyes, and tight grey curls, she looks like a boxer who has had a lot of fights that went the distance and lost most of them.

To say she likes a drink is a massive understatement. When she isn't drinking alcohol, she's making it, producing eye-watering, throat-searing hooch in a still that bubbles away in the bedroom she shares with her mother. She claims its soothing noise helps her get to sleep at night.

"Lissen up real good, Colonel," she tells him. "Ah ain't happy a-wastin' mah precious time a-hangin' around an' watchin' that stupid monkey make a fine ole mess with all them cans o' paint. Ah gotta whole lot better things ter do."

"All I'm asking you to do is make sure he paints some pictures and uses lots of blue. Remember, blue paint; that's important."

"Blue! Wot fer? An' wot's in it fer me?"

"Okay, Aunt Delta, here's the deal. There'll be a big bonus coming your way."

"Ah surely do want that in writin'."

"Don't you trust me?"

"No."

During the coming days, under her supervision, Scatter produces paintings nearly as quickly as General Motors does cars. A stockpile accumulates of canvases covered mainly in blue, and with splashes and zig-zag lines of other vivid colours; some also feature prints of his hands and in one case his knobbly bottom.

"I'm amazed," declares Elvis, standing by the open door of the shed. "This is fantastic, Aunt Delta. Look how many paintings he's done, and they're pretty good. I can see blue must be his favourite colour."

She is reclining on the sofa bed bequeathed by Vernon, drinking a colourless liquid from a glass as large as a flower vase.

Elvis nods towards Scatter, asleep in a corner of the shed and comments, "I guess the little guy has earned a rest. What a change there's been. I suppose he's come to see the value of taking up a hobby like painting to keep him occupied. Congratulations. How've you done it?"

She winks and raises her glass as if in a toast and says they have evolved a routine that suits them both. And leaves it at that.

Elvis is stunned how, having initially agreed it would be a good idea to display some of Scatter's paintings, it has since escalated into a full-blown exhibition at the Peabody Hotel in Memphis.

"I thought we were going to hang a few pictures in the Jungle Room for a week or two, and that would be it," he continues. "Nothing fancy, and it seems to be the right place for them."

"I was thinking along exactly the same lines," agrees the Colonel, while keeping a perfectly straight face.

"But I decided to ask an art expert from Agatha & Christie's to look at the paintings, just in case, and he was astonished by their quality. Of course, I didn't mention they were done by a monkey. He said they were the work of a major new artist."

Elvis looks puzzled and strokes his chin, trying to recall why he'd heard nothing about this art expert before. "Where was I when all this happened?"

"I'm not sure, son, but I knew you'd want me take care of business and do my best for the little guy."

"And the prices put on the paintings – it's incredible. They're for thousands of dollars each!"

"Market forces," says the Colonel with a shrug. "That's what the expert from Agatha & Christie's recommended and who am I to argue."

Elvis and Priscilla greet the guests as they arrive at the first viewing of the exhibition of Scatter's paintings at the Peabody. They include movie producer Hal Wallis; Dean Martin, having been assured there's a free bar; and Liberace, his mother, Frances, and Brother George who, in a nod to the importance of the occasion, has brought along their finest Louis XlV candelabrum.

Elvis is in his iconic Sunburst jumpsuit, and Priscilla wears a chic black suit made for her by top Hollywood designer Edith Head. Scatter, led into the room by Charlie, wears a morning suit with tails, cravat, and a grey top hat which he doffs in acknowledgement of the polite applause.

Canapes and champagne are served to the guests as they read the catalogue and circulate looking at the 50 paintings hung on the walls. The blurb states that the exhibition displays "the perfect fusion of art and music". The dominance of one particular colour throughout the oeuvre is because, like Picasso at the beginning of the 20th century, Scatter has also had a 'blue period'.

It comments that Scatter was constantly drawn to using different shades of blue while inspired by listening to the songs of Elvis, such as *Blue Suede Shoes*, clearly a much-loved favourite, of which there are five different paintings; *Blue Moon of Kentucky* (three versions); and others including *Blue Hawaii*, *Blue Moon*, *Blue Christmas*, and *Blueberry Hill*.

Priscilla takes Liberace by the arm and leads him to one painting called *Indescribably Blue*. "Lee, I've put a reserved sticker on this one, to keep it especially for you," she confides. "Can you see how those black and white flashes against the deep blue background resemble piano keys, and that patch of gold, that could be the Steinway logo, the make of the piano."

Liberace flutters his hands in excitement. "Oh, Priscilla, you're so right. I must show Mommy and my brother George. They'll love it and I know just the place to put it in our home."

Elvis wanders over to join Colonel Parker, and having remarked on how well the exhibition is going, he nods towards Scatter sitting quietly on a chair, eating a sandwich, and seemingly at peace with the world.

"He's been really well behaved today," he goes on. "It's so unlike him in many ways, almost as if he's a different chimpanzee."

"He's probably just a bit overwhelmed by it all, what with it being his first foray into the world of art, and that's what's made him quiet," he replies, sensing that he's been rumbled, and the game is up.

"Have you noticed how that large nick in his left ear has magically disappeared? Is there something you want to tell me, Colonel?"

"You're right, Elvis. You've spotted the switch, an innocent ruse. I was in a dilemma. With all the important guests we've invited, I didn't want to run the risk of Scatter kicking off, causing a riot, and ruining everything."

Colonel Parker isn't going to mention it, but he's already made his mind up to organise another exhibition, as well as arranging some private commissions with celebrity patrons. He can practically feel those cheques with lots of noughts on them tingling in his fingers.

"Do you remember Cheeta the chimp who used to appear in all the

Tarzan films? He fronts an agency that trains chimpanzees for the movies, and I hired the best-behaved one they had on their books."

"Bubba, I'm travelling first class all the way," Colonel Parker calls out across the office to his assistant.

"I assume, sir, that the art exhibition went very well."

"Much better than expected," he answers. Bonhomie radiates like a sunbeam from behind his desk. "It was a triumph. Every picture was sold. The good ole Colonel has done it again!"

"How was Scatter, sir, or should I say the agency chimpanzee? Did anyone notice?"

"Yes, Elvis did, but nobody else. It worked like a charm. The double was better behaved than some of the guests. Listen, I want you to book a limousine to collect me from Graceland, then a first-class flight from Memphis to Las Vegas, and then the President Nixon suite at the International."

He reaches into the pocket of his jacket and holds up a grubby-looking rabbit's foot. "It's practically talking to me. It's saying a big win is coming my way."

"It might also be saying that it could do with a wash," says his assistant. "It's giving off a funny smell."

"Bubba, are you mad! I mustn't wash away the magic, not now I'm so close. As my old friend Ethel Merman says, 'Everything's Coming up Roses'."

There's a knock on the door.

"Ah, that'll be Elvis. He said he wants to talk about the exhibition."

He walks in accompanied by a middle-aged man in a grey suit, rimless glasses and carrying a black leather briefcase, whom neither the Colonel nor Bubba have seen before.

"Colonel, sir, I'd like to go through with you about the money that was received for the paintings."

"No need to worry, son, it's all taken care of. Who's this you've brought with you?"

"This is Mr Silas Catchitt of the attorneys Catchitt and Kyll, of New York."

The lawyer nods towards Colonel Parker and Bubba in turn.

Elvis continues: "I was talking to Lee (Liberace) at the exhibition, and he said I should have a chat with his lawyer and get some independent advice. And that's what I've done. Now, I'd like to talk about the distribution of the money from the sale of the paintings."

The Colonel's previous happy-go-lucky expression has been replaced by one of suspicion. He has also just heard uttered two words he finds extremely unpleasant: 'lawyer' and 'independent'. A hot flush surges through his body like an eruption of the Old Faithful geyser in the Yellowstone National Park. He pulls out an old handkerchief from the sleeve of his jacket to mop his damp, red face, and pushes his straw trilby to the back of his head.

What is Elvis doing? he thinks to himself. *He knows I always take care of business. In the Colonel we trust – that's been the basis of our relationship for nearly twenty years. Now he turns up with some hotshot attorney.*

"I understand that the sales came to about $250,000," notes Elvis.

"Yes, it's business as usual. Under the terms of our contract the money, once expenses have been met, will be shared between us," answers Colonel Parker, nervously glancing at the lawyer who is making a lot of notes on his legal pad.

The attorney puckers his mouth, as if he is sucking on an acid drop before he responds: "Unfortunately, Colonel Parker, that's not the case in this particular instance. As far as my client is concerned, Scatter is his pet, and wholly owned by him. That means he has full responsibility for all things pertaining to this chimpanzee. Therefore, it is Mr Presley's wish that all proceeds from the exhibition should go into a trust fund set up in his name."

The Colonel laughs bitterly. "Do my ears deceive me – a trust fund for a monkey with the brains of a dung beetle? What's happened to our contract that says we always split everything fifty-fifty? Elvis, what's going on?"

Mr Catchitt removes his glasses to give them a polish on a spotlessly clean white handkerchief.

He resumes: "I've been looking at the various contracts signed by my client and yourself, including the one from August 1955 when, I should point out, my client was only twenty years old; the amended version signed in March 1956; and the one concerning special projects that was signed in May 1963. None of these contracts cover such things as this art exhibition and its proceeds.

"We have scrutinized them carefully and offered our advice to Mr Presley; however, it is his express wish that all other business arrangements between yourselves should continue as before."

After Elvis and his attorney have left, Colonel Parker remains slumped in his chair, like a burst Zeppelin that has collapsed slowly to the ground. Finally, with a sad shake of the head, he brushes away the accumulated cigar ash from the front of his orange Hawaiian shirt.

"All that I've done for that boy!" He noisily blows his nose on his handkerchief. "And what do I get? I've been trussed up like a turkey at Thanksgiving." There is a clunk as his lucky rabbit's foot lands in the wastepaper bin.

"To be fair, sir, the attorney did explain that all your other contracts with Elvis are not affected," comments his assistant, "and they're the ones that matter. It's only the paintings they're talking about, and in the scale of things, sir, the amount of money involved is chicken feed. By the way, do you want me to continue making the arrangements for your trip to Las Vegas?"

"Don't mock, Bubba. How can I go when my stake has just been handed to a monkey! But your comment about chicken feed has got me thinking."

For the next hour his assistant cannot be sure if the Colonel, sitting motionless in his chair, is concentrating very hard or fast asleep. In the meantime, he carries on with inserting rejection slips into envelopes to be mailed back to suppliers with their invoices.

Colonel Parker emerges from his hibernation, looking very pleased with himself to declare: "Two can play at this game."

"What game is that, sir?" inquires Bubba. "I didn't know you were a sportsman."

"Very funny. Leave the jokes to Jack Benny. Tell me, Bubba, would you call the Dixie Chickens my pets?"

"Well, sir, they're not like a puppy or a hamster, are they? They're a troupe of dancing chickens – a vaudeville act is how I'd describe them."

"Vaudeville!" he snorts. "You're being a bit hard, Bubba. Artistes is how I'd refer to them. Their fans will tell you the Radio City Rockettes and the Bluebell Girls have nothing on the Dixie Chickens. But you do agree they belong solely to me and are not part of the EPCP Enterprises contract I have with Elvis?"

His assistant, who concedes the point, has an uneasy feeling where this is heading. And he's right. The Colonel wants to organise an art exhibition of paintings done by the Dixie Chickens.

As far as his assistant is concerned, there is one major flaw in the concept: How can a chicken paint?

But the Colonel has it all figured out. He explains: "There are five of them, so we dip their feet into ten different colours. Then we put a blank canvas on top of a hot plate and play *Sweet Georgia Brown*. The

Dixie Chickens will think it is their usual routine and start hopping about. What do we get? Art!"

He says he will talk to Elvis about using Scatter's studio and to Aunt Delta to handle the painting side of things, bearing in mind the success she had in getting the best out of the chimp.

"I'm thinking that the theme of the exhibition will be 'Songs from the Shows'," he continues. "They'll paint while they dance to songs from musicals like *Calamity Jane* and *The King and I*."

"Thank goodness I retrieved my lucky rabbit's foot from the wastepaper bin," he tells Elvis and Bubba a few days later. "One rub and the old magic returned."

He announces that he needs to leave for Las Vegas on a potential win-win business mission. "That is, if Elvis can spare me for a few days," he adds. The Colonel notes that he doesn't take long to consider this, before agreeing.

While he's there he'll talk to a producer concerning a part for Elvis in a disaster movie about the world's tallest building catching fire.

"I know you've not died in any of your films since *Love Me Tender*, and he wants me to assure you, Elvis, that you'll be one of those who escapes; you won't be so much as singed in this one."

"At least it won't be another musical comedy like the other thirty-one movies I've done," comments Elvis. "It'll be a relief to do something like this, to act and not have to sing an album's worth of mechanically produced songs. Yes, I'm interested."

He groans when his manager replies that the producer is hoping to include at least two. They'd be a major selling point for the movie.

Colonel Parker goes on to reveal that the art world will have to wait for the first exhibition of paintings by the Dixie Chickens.

"That is sad news, sir," says Bubba, "but you don't seem in the least bit disappointed."

"We've been overtaken by events," he says. He pauses to light a celebratory Walmart Havana-style cigar, before explaining that he's heard from a company that plans to open a chain of fried chicken restaurants throughout the South, and they want to engage the Dixie Chickens as their poster girls, to feature in commercials, perform at certain restaurants and help open new ones.

"This could relaunch their career on a whole new level," he beams. "Who knows where it could end – TV, the movies!" He attempts to blow a smoke ring but merely produces a dark, dense cloud that looks like it could herald a thunderstorm.

Elvis inquires: "But what about your old friend Colonel Harland Sanders? Won't he be upset, after all the promotion work the Dixie Chickens have done for Kentucky Fried Chicken in the past?"

"Yes, he's the first person I'll call when I've heard the proposals from the new restaurant chain. I'm expecting to start a bidding war."

THAT'S ALL RIGHT

Elvis pulls back the flap of the tent and pauses while his eyes adjust to the darkness of the interior. "Madam Destiny?" he inquires. A red light, suspended from a pole, switches on and a quavery voice tells him, "Come in, sir, you seeker after truth."

Sitting at the far side of the table is an ancient gipsy woman who Elvis reckons must be one of the oldest living things in America; in terms of age, she'd probably give the giant redwoods a run for their money.

Her skin is grey and creased like an old newspaper, her eyes are watery, and her thin, greasy grey hair hangs like rats' tails on her shoulders. A bony, ring-covered hand pulls away a velvet cloth to reveal a crystal ball in the centre of the table. "Sit there opposite me and don't say a word," she croaks. "The spirits will tell me all I need to know."

Elvis and the guys are visiting the Memphis Cotton Carnival, so he's decided to dress for the occasion in a white jumpsuit with a picture of a Fender guitar on the chest, and musical notes picked out in brightly coloured crystals on the arms and flared trousers. His outfit is completed by a short purple lined cape and a large belt buckle with an image of a drum kit.

Usually, unless he is heavily disguised, the sight of Elvis walking around Memphis would attract a frenzy of fans, all wanting to greet the King, with the result that downtown would become gridlocked. But there's no need for such precautions today. It's carnival and lots of people are wearing fancy dress; he's already seen at least 50 men dressed as Vegas Elvis, so nobody is going to know who is the real one.

"I'm hiding in plain sight," he tells Charlie Hodge, Red and Sonny West, and Lamar Fike, members of the Memphis Mafia, who live with him at Graceland, as they follow the parade of floats, brass bands, jazz bands, and baton-twirling majorettes as it makes its way down Main Street.

Afterwards they mingle with the crowds walking along the midway lined with amusement rides, food vendors, animal acts and dime stores. It's a happy stroll down Memory Lane for Elvis, who hasn't been to the Cotton Carnival for many years.

"I wonder if Colonel Parker is here," laughs Elvis. "He'd love it. He'd be right at home. He first started in carny with a dancing chickens act. He had them hopping about on a hot plate covered in straw. Can you believe it! He's still managing the same act today – called the Dixie Chickens."

They've only been there half an hour and already Lamar Fike has visited three food vendors and demolished helpings of corn dogs, funnel cake fries, and barbecue turkey legs as if they were hors d'oeuvres at a cocktail party.

Charlie points out he should visit the tent of Lady Gargantua, billed as America's fattest lady, for his opinion of her size. He's reluctant because he's seen a stall selling toffee apples and candy floss that he'd much rather visit. Having been promised he can go there next, he agrees to take a look.

"She's slim pickings," is the dismissive verdict of the second fattest man in America, who is beaten only by Elvis's record producer Steve Sholes, someone so enormous that his wife uses his trouser belt as a washing line.

"She's no more than chubby," he sneers. "It was a poor show all round. The fat lady didn't even sing. Toffee apples, anyone?"

Afterwards the guys come across the tent of Madam Destiny and Elvis is dared to find out what fate has in store for him. He agrees, remarking that it will be interesting to compare Madam Destiny's vision of his future with that of his manager, Colonel Tom Parker.

"I'm betting it will be another film produced by Hal Wallis with ten songs for the album tie-in, and the movie will be in the can from start to finish in no more than three weeks," laughs Red West. "After all, it's June and you've only released two movies so far this year. You could get in another couple before the end of the year."

"No," grins his cousin, Sonny. "The future I see is another season at the International Hotel in Las Vegas, only longer than the last one."

Elvis sits down and asks if he should he cross her palm with silver. "No," cackles the old crone, holding out a claw-like hand that resembles a turkey foot. "It's ten dollars."

Her hands hover over the crystal ball as if she is warming them. She studies Elvis for several seconds, closes her eyes and begins to moan quietly, moving her head slowly from side to side.

"Are you all right, Ma'am?" he inquires.

She opens one rheumy eye for a second or two and rasps: "Don't be alarmed, good sir. I'm going into my trance. Some people are faith healers – I'm a fate healer."

More moans and swaying while her hands flutter over the crystal ball. "The spirits are telling me that you are in show business."

Elvis feigns to be surprised. "Remarkable. That's absolutely true."

There's more moaning and after a furtive peep at Elvis, Madam Destiny announces, "You are also closely connected with music."

"Well, I do declare," answers Elvis, slapping his thigh. "That's amazing! Only the spirits could have known that! I'm very impressed, Madam Destiny. Thank goodness I came to see you. What else do the spirits say?"

She appears to be inured to his sarcasm. The moaning has become a wail, and the old gipsy is rocking backwards and forwards in her chair. She raises her arms – thin as a spider's legs – and calls out: "The spirits say you should do all you can to help an old man who has done so much for your career."

Elvis asks: "Does the crystal ball reveal who this old man is and what help he needs?"

She shakes her head. "No, it has gone cloudy."

"That's a pity," he declares. As he gets up to go, she says she has something for him. She rummages in the pocket of her dress before pulling out a sprig of white heather and handing it to him. It is dried out and looks nearly as old as she does. "It'll bring you good luck, kind sir." Her smile reveals that she doesn't have many teeth left.

"Okay, thanks. You're the fortune teller. You must think I need it," he comments.

The old gipsy holds out a cupped hand: "That'll be another ten bucks, sir." She tucks it into her purse where it joins the other note. He can hear her cackling to herself as he leaves the tent.

The guys huddle round Elvis, eager to find out what the fortune teller told him. He believes she must be an old associate of the Colonel's from his time in carny. "She said I must do all I can to help an old man who has done a lot for my career," he reports. "She didn't say who it is, but we can all guess who she means."

Yes, they all nod in agreement: Colonel Parker.

"The whole thing cost me twenty dollars," says Elvis ruefully. There is a sharp intake of breath from the Memphis Mafia. "That included a piece of lucky white heather, but it looked so mangy I threw it away."

"Was that wise, King?" wonders Charlie. "It might invoke a gipsy's curse and bring you bad luck."

A few days later Elvis is waiting in his white Lincoln Continental parked outside Schwab's store on Beale Street while Charlie has gone inside to pick up some household cleaning supplies. It has only been a couple of minutes but already Elvis is looking anxiously at his watch and drumming his fingers on the steering wheel. What's taking him so long, he frets.

Charlie, one of whose jobs is to keep Graceland clean and tidy, is running low on dusters, furniture polish and window cleaner spray. But the main reason for the visit is he wants to try on a new apron with a deep pocket at the front that's being displayed on a mannequin in the store; it will be an upgrade on his now faded floral pinafore.

He emerges onto the sidewalk wearing an apron. "What do you think, El – this blue one or should I get the pink?"

"Get them both and let's hustle, Charlie," he urges, holding his arm aloft and pointing at his watch.

Elvis is impatient because he, too, wants to try on something new – an outfit that Bernard Lansky is working on for the opening night of his new season at the International Hotel in Las Vegas. He hasn't seen it yet, but the man who has been designing his outfits since his days at Sun, has described it as sensational.

The image on the chest of the jumpsuit features a phoenix rising from the flames; but, according to Bernard Lansky, what makes it so special is that when the spotlights hit Elvis as he stands centre stage and pulls back his cape to reveal the image, the coloured crystals, rhinestones, and sequins worked into the design will make it look as if he is on fire. There are also dazzling flashes of flames on the arms and along the seams of the flared trousers.

Elvis can visualize the impact it will have on the audience: it will be stunning. The King of Rock and Roll becomes the King of Fire: he'll stand there for fully a minute, arms spread wide, not moving, his body seemingly ablaze, while they shout his name. Then with an imperceptible signal to the band he'll tear into the opening number – *Burning Love* – and his fans will go wild. Bernard Lansky is right: it will be sensational, and he can't wait to try it on.

As soon as Charlie has loaded his supplies into the car, Elvis is striding along Beale Street towards Lansky's outfitters store. Suddenly he stops.

"Hey, I know that voice," he tells Charlie. "I'd know it anywhere."

"Whoever it is, he's singing one of your songs – *That's All Right*."

"No, Charlie, it's one of his songs."

Elvis walks right past Lansky's until he is standing next to an old man who is singing and playing his guitar on the sidewalk outside the Gut Bucket Blues Club.

"Hello, Arthur, er... Mr Crudup, sir. What are you doing here?" He shakes his gnarled hand and gives him a hug. "Somebody as good as you should be playing in clubs and theatres, not on a street corner."

"Good to see you again, Elvis," he replies. "It's been a mighty long time. Lordy, I don't know how many years it's been. But these be hard times, and I've come to Memphis to stand here and sing my songs to earn a few dollars."

On the ground is a battered old guitar case with a few coins scattered inside. Clearly, he hasn't been having much success.

He stands hunched with age, his hair and eyebrows are white, and he is dressed in a grubby, collarless shirt, denim dungarees, sandals, and no socks. The joints of his hands are swollen with arthritis and Elvis realises it must be painful to play his cheap-looking acoustic guitar. Always known as 'Big Boy', Elvis regards him as one of the finest of all blues singers; he is desperately sad to see how he has been shrunk by poverty.

He insists on taking him to a diner with himself and Charlie for a steak, apple pie and a coffee. And he waits until he's finished before saying anything.

Elvis remarks: "Do you know what I used to say when I was a boy? I want to be a singer as good as Arthur 'Big Boy' Crudup. That was my ambition, to try and be like you. You should be retired and living in comfort, not performing on street corners. How can I help you? How can I repay you for what you've done for me with your songs like *That's All Right*, *My Baby Left Me* and *So Glad You're Mine*?"

Elvis remembers the words told to him by Madam Destiny, the old gipsy fortune teller, at the Cotton Carnival a few days ago: "The spirits say you should do all you can to help an old man who has done so much for your career." She was right, but it wasn't Colonel Parker, his manager, that she meant – it was Arthur 'Big Boy' Crudup! Now that he understands, he will make it his mission to save him.

He explains that he came to Memphis, the home of the blues and where better, to try and make some money because he didn't know what else to do. He's behind with the rent, and he needs medical treatment. "The trouble is I'm flat broke."

Charlie asks him about the royalties he receives for all the great songs he wrote, and which Elvis still includes in his act. Surely, they must be a big help financially.

He laughs without humour and shakes his head in resignation as his eyes fill with tears. "In all the years I've been performing, I've never received a cent for any of the songs I wrote. Not one cent."

Elvis is incredulous. "But that's impossible. You've written so many."

"It's true. Not one cent."

He recounts how a friend has been trying to negotiate an agreement for back royalties that will see him being paid $60,000. But it has taken years to get this far; however, the music publishers, Hoot & Nanny, from whom he is supposed to get the royalties, have still not signed the legal documents. And until that happens, he won't receive any money.

"That's a coincidence," comments Elvis, "because they also happen to publish most of my songs. I'll go and see them, and I reckon we can soon sort this out.

"In the meantime, you're coming back to Graceland with us. Dr Nick, my personal physician, will take care of you and make sure you're well, and my grandmother, Minnie Mae, she'll build up your strength with her down-home cooking. You couldn't be in better hands, Mr Crudup. I'm so glad we met you today because I believe your luck has just changed."

Charlie is too loyal to say anything to Elvis, but he wonders how the old blues singer will get on being cared for at Graceland; he's known perfectly fit young men buckle under the ministrations of Dr Nick, Aunt Delta and Minnie Mae.

Arthur Crudup spends most of his first 48 hours at Graceland fast asleep in the small one-bed hospital that Dr Nick has next to his office-cum-pharmacy, tended by Aunt Delta, acting as his nurse. She sits on a chair in the corner, smoking roll-up cigarettes, wearing a grubby apron with a red cross, and accompanied by her mobile cocktail cabinet – a fully fitted-out suitcase on wheels with an extendable handle.

As a rule, Aunt Delta finds that patients cause the least problems and disruption to her routine if they are asleep. Consequently, some of the potions she administers to the blues singer contain her homemade moonshine, which is as effective as any anaesthetic.

When Elvis calls in to see how he's doing, he swats away the overhanging cloud of smoke and complains that the room smells like a bar. "Don't tell me, Aunt Delta. Let me guess what you've been giving him."

"Ah'm a-sayin' plenty o' rest be the best cure fer a patient, an' that be wut he's a-gettin'," she declares, as she stubs out her cigarette in a petri dish, miffed at Elvis's criticism of her care programme. If there were ever to be a Fifth Horseman of the Apocalypse, then it would be Aunt Delta in a nurse's uniform.

He is pleased to note that, true to form, Dr Nick has been busy with his prescription pad, and there are several bottles of pills of different colours on the bedside cabinet.

Meanwhile, Priscilla has advised Minnie Mae that soups and stews are the best form of nourishment for a patient, particularly one in such a frail state of health, and that she should avoid giving him such things as deep fried battered chitlins and alligator pies.

"Ah knows jest the thing to perk him up," says Elvis's grandmother. But even Arthur Crudup, who is by no means a picky eater, is surprised to see a catfish head, whiskers and all, looking up at him from his bowl of soup, surrounded by lumps of turnip. It makes up his mind to suggest to Elvis, as politely as he can, bearing in mind all the help that he is receiving at Graceland, that he should find a place of his own as soon as he receives the royalties he's due from Hoot & Nanny.

Before setting off for Nashville to press the music publishers to pay up, Elvis asks his manager if he can help find him somewhere.

Colonel Parker puts on his sorrowful face and comments: "This is a charity case, and you know my views about charity. I keep a wastepaper bin in my office especially for begging letters. See, it's nearly full and that's just from today's mail."

"But, Colonel, sir…"

"You believe this is a very deserving case. Because you've promised to help the guy, I might be able to pull a few strings and find somewhere for him very quickly." He turns to his assistant: "Bubba, show Elvis the brochure. It looks perfect."

Elvis is shocked when he sees that it is for the Happy Days Are Here Again RIP home in Florida. "No, Colonel Parker, we can't do this to him and send him to a RIP home. The poor guy will think it's a death sentence."

He is mollified when Bubba explains that RIP means Reside in Perpetuity. "It will be his forever home," he adds.

Nevertheless, Elvis points out, it is a home for retired carny folks, which means he'll be living with the likes of the bearded lady and Sammy the performing seal.

"Elvis, son, these are showbiz people, like Mr Arthur Crudup. Mrs Parker and I love it; we have a week's holiday there every year. He'll feel right at home. And it's in Florida. What's not to like."

But when Elvis continues to grumble and shake his head, his manager holds his hands up in surrender. "All right, I get it. You don't want him to go there. Now what does the good ole Colonel always do?"

"You take care of business, sir."

"Correct. Leave this with me. Go and have your meeting with Hoot & Nanny and see what you can do, while I'll see if there's another way of coming up with an answer to the guy's problems."

It is a long drive to Nashville and Elvis has many hours to brood on the injustice suffered by the blues singer and the part played by the music publisher Hoot & Nanny. By the time he gets there he is so incensed that he marches up to the reception desk and demands to speak immediately to whoever is in charge.

Once she has got over the shock of seeing who it is, the receptionist says that would be Mr Wesley. Does Mr Presley have an appointment because she can see nothing in his diary?

"No, ma'am, but I want to see him right now."

"He's actually in a meeting, Mr Presley."

"I suggest you go and tell him that Elvis Presley is here, and I expect to see him in the next sixty seconds. Or else." He looks down at his watch and begins counting 59-58-57…

He's reached 11 when he looks up and wonders if he has slipped into a time warp and is back in 1950 because it could be Hank Williams himself walking towards him dressed in a light grey single-breasted suit with black treble clefs on the lapels, trousers tucked into tooled cowboy boots, shoelace tie and white Stetson hat. What is he: the head of one of the biggest music publishing businesses in the world or a tribute act?

"Please excuse us, Elvis, we didn't expect you," he says, introducing himself as Ronald Aloysius Wesley IV, president of Hoot & Nanny. "We're honoured that you've come to visit us. Please follow me to my office."

Elvis stays where he is. "What I want to say will be said right here where everyone can hear me."

The president swallows and looks uneasy.

He tells how he came to meet Arthur 'Big Boy' Crudup and the parlous state of his health and finances. With all the wonderful songs he has written he should be living in relative comfort. But no. Incredibly, he has never received a dime in royalties in his entire life. His situation would be so much better if he were to receive the $60,000 in back royalties that has been negotiated on his behalf, but Hoot & Nanny is refusing to sign the legal papers that will release the money.

"Sixty thousand dollars!" he declares, pointing at the president. "For a company this size, it's chicken feed. You must make that much in a month from my recordings and performances alone. Shame on you!"

Everyone in the office has stopped work to listen and they are all watching the president to see how he will react.

He is flustered, his face has gone bright red, and he indicates that Elvis should join him in his office while he talks to their legal people.

Elvis doesn't move. He turns and slowly looks round at everyone and announces: "I'm giving notice that I will never sing or record another Hoot & Nanny song again until that money is paid!"

"But, Elvis, you can't do that. That's a huge part of your repertoire, some of your greatest songs," points out the president, who removes his hat and mops his face. He dearly wishes he hadn't come to work today. Wouldn't it be great if the floor were to suddenly open up beneath him? It is a confrontation he knows he cannot win.

"You're right. But I'll explain the reason why to all my fans and I reckon they will understand and be sympathetic. I'll also talk to all my fellow artistes about the reason for the boycott. I'm betting they will want to follow my example and refuse to perform any Hoot & Nanny material. And they might well join me in a protest demonstration outside your offices. That'll look good on all the TV news channels."

A voice somewhere at the back of the office calls out: "You're right, Elvis. We should pay up and help the guy." There is a round of applause from everyone in the office.

"Okay, President Ron, here's what's going to happen. You have forty-eight hours to sort this out before I start making the calls." He turns and walks out of the office.

"But Elvis, it isn't that simple," he wails.

"You idiot!" Colonel Parker yells down the phone to the president of Hoot & Nanny. "What a mess you've got yourself into over a paltry sixty thousand dollars and now you want me to bail you out! How am I going to do that, Ron? Let me explain. You're on board the Titanic, you've been hit by an iceberg called Elvis, and you're sinking like a stone."

Ronald Aloysius Wesley IV called the Colonel as soon as Elvis left the building. He was there for only 10 minutes but in that time, he'd done enough damage to potentially wreck the biggest name in country music publishing and turn its president into a pariah.

What will his wife say? The board? Wall Street? What will they make of it at the Grand Ole Opry, not forgetting the humiliation of being mocked unmercifully by Minnie Pearl? He'll be jeered out of Nashville. He's frantic, trying to hold back the onrushing flood of disaster with a colander.

The Colonel continues: "The way I see it is that you and your people thought you were dealing with some old guy that nobody had ever heard of. Whatever the rightness of his case, he wasn't important and so he could be ignored. Nothing was done and the money stayed in the bank. Unfortunately for you, Elvis Presley is Arthur 'Big Boy' Crudup's biggest fan, and he believes that the songs of his that he's recorded and performed over the years helped make him the King of Rock and Roll."

"Please, Colonel, as an old friend and business associate, I'm begging you to do whatever you can to save Hoot & Nanny and... yes... me, as well."

Colonel Parker laughs ironically. "You don't know what you're asking. Elvis is madder than a nest of wasps that's been poked with a stick."

The Colonel decides to leave him dangling on the phone for a while. He puffs on his Walmart Havana-style cigar and takes a couple of pulls on the lever of the gaming machine that he keeps next to his desk. Of course, he loses, as he always does. But, like a pig trained to find truffles, he can sniff dollars undetectable to anybody else.

He hears Ron saying in the receiver lying on his desk, "Hello, Colonel Parker, are you still there? Hello... Hello..."

Colonel Parker smirks and rubs his stubbly jowls. He senses there's a jackpot to be won in Nashville and he's going to play President Ron like a violin.

He decides to give the anxiety button a push. "Sorry about that, Ron. I was just having a word with Elvis (who, of course, isn't in his office). I had to tell him to stop making those protest placards; what with all the hammering going on I could hardly hear a word you were saying."

There is a groan from the other end of the phone.

"Look, I'll talk to him," he says, trying hard to sound sympathetic, a quality that's usually alien to him. "But you know how stubborn he can be once he's made up his mind. Oh, wait a minute, Ron, Elvis wants to tell me something. Perhaps he's had a change of heart."

He holds the phone for a minute while unsuccessfully trying to blow smoke rings and brushing away the debris of cigar ash that has scattered down the front of his Hawaiian shirt.

"Sorry, Ron, he just wanted to say that Frank Sinatra, Barbra Streisand, Vice-President Agnew, and Mickey Mouse will be among the celebrities joining him in the demonstration outside the Hoot & Nanny offices. And I know that Hal Wallis is bringing a party of stars from Paramount Studios."

The response is a series of long, agonised groans.

Colonel Parker continues: "If Elvis listens to anybody, it's me. I'll do my very best to salvage what I can of your business and your career."

President Ron is at the end of his tether. "Please tell me what I can do to put things right. Anything!"

There's a long intake of breath from the Colonel as if he is giving the matter a lot of serious thought.

"Here's the plan, Ron," he finally announces, and then pauses, allowing for the tension to build at the other end of the phone. He continues: "To beat Elvis's forty-eight-hour deadline and save you and your business, you must immediately send me the signed legal documents authorising the release of the unpaid royalties to Arthur 'Big Boy' Crudup, plus the sixty thousand dollars he's owed.

"In addition, you're going to pay me another sixty thousand dollars commission for fixing the mess that you and Hoot & Nanny created in the first place. The documents and the one hundred and twenty thousand dollars in cash need to be here at Graceland by noon tomorrow. That's it, Ron. You can take it or leave it."

Silence. Silence that is dragging on far too long for Colonel Parker's liking. He pushes the anxiety button again.

"Hold on a minute, will you, Ron. Elvis wants to tell me something…"

"All right!" he shouts down the phone, so loud that the Colonel yanks it away from his ear. "I'll take it! I'll take the deal!"

Colonel Parker and Bubba, his assistant, join Elvis and Arthur 'Big Boy' Crudup in the Jungle Room. The old blues singer is sitting in one of the faux fur-covered armchairs, smiling and looking relaxed. The Colonel is surprised but pleased to see how well he has come through being treated by Dr Nick, tended by Aunt Delta, and fed by Minnie Mae. He looks a lot fitter and a lot smarter; his old dungarees and sandals having been replaced by jacket, shirt, slacks, and highly polished shoes. Debonair is the word that comes to mind, and it is such a contrast to how he was when Elvis found him busking on a corner in Beale Street.

"I have some good news," he announces, placing a briefcase on a coffee table.

"The royalties due to Mr Crudup are much more than was thought," he continues. "Hoot & Nanny have had another look at the figures and factored in the interest that was due, and taking all things into consideration, the final amount comes to one hundred and twenty thousand dollars. That's double the original figure."

"Wow!" exclaims Elvis.

Arthur Crudup takes out a handkerchief and dabs his eyes and noisily blows his nose. He shakes his head, as if trying to make sense of what he has been told and how his life will be transformed.

Colonel Parker hands him the signed legal documents and shows him the inside of the briefcase that's filled with stacks of dollar bills.

"You'll see that the papers confirm that payments of royalties on your songs will be made to you regularly in future."

He appears overwhelmed. He sits gently rocking backwards and forwards in the chair before mumbling, "Thank you, sir. I'm dreaming. After all those years of hardship, I don't know what to say."

"We need to thank Elvis," replies Colonel Parker. "He brought you to Graceland and then he went to see Hoot & Nanny to convince them of the justice of your case and that they should release the money as soon as possible. It's all down to Elvis who made them see sense at last."

There are tears in his eyes as Arthur Crudup walks over to shake Elvis's hand.

Colonel Parker never mentions his own role in the affair or the extra $60,000 that he extracted from the music publishers, either then or afterwards. It remained a secret. Perhaps he saw it as an act of charity, something quite out of character with his often-expressed hardline views on so-called worthy causes, and therefore it needed to be suppressed. The last thing he wanted was for anyone to think he was a bit of a softie. But he understood why Elvis felt he owed so much to the old blues singer.

Elvis has arranged for a limousine to take the blues singer to Memphis airport for a journey that will end in Nassawadox, Virginia, where he has lived for the past few years and where he will move into a new apartment. He says he'd rather stay there, where he has put down roots, than move to the home for retired showbiz people in Florida suggested by Colonel Parker.

He stands on the steps to say goodbye to everyone at Graceland who have turned his life around. He shakes Elvis's hand first and then completes a circuit of the others. Minnie Mae hands him a packed lunch that she's made for the trip. He thanks her but decides against asking what it contains. It's better not to know.

"I owe you all so much," he says, trying hard not to get emotional. "I can think of only one way of repaying you. When I'm settled in my new home, I'm going to write a new song for Elvis, something as good as *That's All Right*. It will be my gift."

He never did, but it was a nice thought.